NO ONE IS SAFE AT NIGHT

A KILLER IS ON THE LOOSE

JELL BARKER

Ordering Information:

Prime Seven Media
518 Landmann St.
Tomah City, WI 54660

Printed in the United States of America

TABLE OF CONTENTS

THE LIVES OF THREE FRIENDS

A VA, ALLY, AND IVY have all been friends since high school, all living in the suburb of Lake Falls.

They dated guys from the same friend group growing up, and are now in there mid – 20's. They all work together at an adult dance club in the city, working the night life.

On a beautiful summers day on February 3rd Ava organised a lunch so the girls could catch up at Café Luz on the beachside.

The sun was shining, and people passed by as they sat out on a street table waiting for their orders. The slight breeze which passed through was just enough to cool them all slightly.

Ava was telling Ally and Ivy that her boyfriend, Jax, proposed. She was so happy to tell her best friends the great news.

Ivy and Ally were so happy for Ava. They all started talking everything and anything to do with weddings.

Time passed and Ava, Ally and Ivy finished lunch. They decided to go home to have rest before they went to work at 7pm.

Arriving at their work "Dance for Me" they met in their dressing rooms, still excited from Ava's good news. They put on their makeup, did their hair and got dressed to go out and perform in the hope they would make enough income for the night. All the while they were discussing their next catch up, deciding it should be a makeover the following week so that they could get their nails, hair, makeup and tanning done Ivy decided to book it all and pay for Ava as a gift to celebrate her good news.

7pm came around so the girls entered the main floor and began to work. The music was pumping and all the girls were dancing to attract attention so that they could dance for customers. It was a Friday night and extremely busy. Groups of men were booked in for buck's nights and work celebrations, then there was groups just there to relax and have some fun.

Later during the night Ava's fiancé Jax came in with friends to surprise Ava at work. She was busy with customers but made eye contact with her favourite man, Jax.

They grabbed a drink from the bar and sat to chill for the night. Meanwhile, Ivy and Ally were doing a double act for a group of police officers that were on a buck's night. There were eight policemen, off-duty of course, sitting there happy drinking, watching Ivy and Ally dance, and were paying large tips for the girls to continue for longer than they should. At the end of the performance Ivy approached Ally and asked her if she felt weird about one of the guys, his persona and the way he watched them.

Ally didn't seem to take too much notice, so Ivy blew it off.

It was time for the three girls to have a break, so they sat with Jax and his friends. One of the friends was on his phone and a Breaking News notification appeared on his phone stating "another woman has been found murdered."

Over the last six months women were going missing or had been found murdered and their bodies were disposed of throughout Mount Macedon ranges, although they are taken from the suburbs of Melbourne by a madman.

This sparked a conversation between the group and the girls were saying they need not panic but be alert and wary of those who they are with and try to stay together when they could. Jax and his friends waited for the girls to finish work for the night and they all said goodbye to each other and went home – a good night had by all.

Life went on as normal, the girls caught up for their makeover day and left feeling amazing – new, fresh and ready to hit work with a new sense of confidence.

A couple of days passed and the girls were wedding shopping at the mall. They passed a TV shop and noticed the news was on, it said the name of the woman found was Kia Hope. The coroner said that Kia's fingertips and teeth were removed, but they had other DNA evidence. She was 23 years old and her mother reported her missing a month ago to the police, but they blew her off saying she probably left intentionally. Although they made a report suggesting Kia was missing, it was not followed through.

The girls stood in silence for a moment, processing what they had just heard. As they walked into the wedding shop all they could hear was passer-by's whispering about Kia and how sad they were for the family.

*　*　*

ON JAX'S BUCK'S NIGHT he and his friends all decided instead they wanted to go camping on the Murray River and just be boys.

But the girls wanted to take Ava to dinner and then dancing then they moved on to a male adult entertainment venue.

With several drinks in hand, they were relaxed and happy. They enjoyed the male's dressing up to perform their dances, and one of the dancers was dressed up in a fireman's outfit.

Ivy asked Ally 'look at that man, does he look familiar to you?'

Ally stared hard, she had had more than six drinks, but said 'yes, but I do not know where from.' Other performers came out and they soon forgot about the fireman dancer until there was an interval where all the dancers could mingle with the women. The fireman dancer saw Ava with her bride sash on and approached the group.

'Hello,' he said. 'My name is Rise, nice to meet you all.'

Ava smiled and returned the greeting, as did Ally and Ivy, but with suspicion on their face as they knew they had seen him somewhere but could not recall. Rise ordered the girls another round of drinks and conversation got started. Rise was saying he was a policeman during work hours and a performance dancer on weekends and since he is a policeman, he wanted to wear a fireman's outfit for his dance shows.

Ivy's face dropped and she pulled Ally to the side. She said 'that's it! He's one of the guys that came into work in that group of policemen that had the buck's night. I asked you if you felt he was looking at us strange.' Ally appeared to be remembering and said, 'yes, I do remember his face now, what are the chances we see him again?'

Rise said to the girls, 'If you wait till after the show, I will be happy to walk you all to the car with what is going on around Melbourne. With women missing and being murdered and all.' The girls all agreed to wait as they thought it was a nice gesture coming from a real police officer. It was nearly 1am and Ava had had an awesome night. Rise came over to them and they left the venue, as he walked them to the car he was asking, 'where do you girls need to drive to? Where's home?'

'Lake Falls,' they replied.

He said, 'oh, that is not too far. Best get going.' Unbeknownst to the girls, Rise memorised their number plate.

* * *

MARCH THE 7ᵀᴴ CAME, the grand wedding day for Ava and Jax. Ivy and Ally stayed with Ava the night before the wedding, as Ivy was the Matron of Honour and Ally was a bridesmaid. The sun was shining, there was no wind, no rain, the birds were singing. The girls had a champagne breakfast with chicken while waiting for the hairdresser and makeup artist.

The doorbell rang but they didn't hear it due to the music being too loud. They opened the door and it was a florist. Ava's was surprised with joy, but she was wondering who they were from. Reading the little note, it said "to my wife to be can't wait to see your smiling face next to mine. Love Jax."

Ava's face was glowing, Ivy and Ally were so happy for her and hoped that one day they would have the same fairy-tale.

The doorbell rang again 30 minutes later, Ava opened the door and saw the girls' puzzled expression. It was more flowers not handed to her, but placed on the doorstep. Ava looked down at the flowers and then looked around to try to see if anybody was there but couldn't see anyone. Ava brought them inside and they were beautiful. The girls were all making a fuss, asking, 'who were they from? Read the note!'

But there was no note, and Ava did not know who they were from.

Ava kept on getting ready for her big day. She looked gorgeous in her white wedding dress with a halter neck, low back, and scattered sequence to highlight the dress in the light. Ivy and Ally came out from the other rooms dressed to impress in their silver, formal, low-cleavage, off-the-shoulder, fitted long dresses with a high split up to the thigh. Looking sexy but elegant, their long curls draping their neckline.

The ceremony proceeded without a hitch. Ava and Jax are now married and more in love than ever.

They went off to get their photos taken at the botanic gardens for an hour. People in the gardens were all staring at them and admiring how great they looked, and people were taking their own photos of the happy couple. They then moved onto the reception venue, called Wedding Bliss. It was stunning, with table centre pieces made of wildflowers, white chair covers, and chandeliers sparkling from the roof. The theme of silver was throughout the venue and everything sparkled.

Food and drinks came out, music played, and the wedding couple had their wedding dance to Adele's Make You Feel My Love. Speeches were made, laughs were had, and a sensational night had by all.

All the family and guests headed to their cars to go home for the night, but not before they had to pass a breath test. Ally and Ivy got a lift home from Jax's friends Tate and Blade. It was Tate and Blade's turn to have the test, both Ally and Ivy sat in the back seat. They looked out the window at the officer who was producing the test and they looked at each other in disbelief as they realised it was Rise, from the Hen's night they met at the club.

As Rise looked in the car at the passengers, he saw the girls in the back and said hi to them. They froze, thinking how could this be? It was the third time they had seen this man, in a soft spoken voice they said, 'hello.' Blade drove off as he passed the test and they all went home.

Ava and Jax had taken time off work so they went away, just for a week to the Maldives for a little honeymoon, then they were going to go back to work when they got back.

Meanwhile, Ivy and Ally returned to work and continued on with life while waiting for their friend to return.

It was a Wednesday night and Ivy was not feeling well, so she stayed home, didn't go to work, and rang Ally to tell her. Ally said that she would check in with her tomorrow.

Ally went to work and it was not too busy, but busy enough with the businesspeople coming in for a mid-week wind down. The end of Ally's shift came, so she said goodbye to security at the entry door and they said, 'Good night, Ally, be safe and drive carefully. See you tomorrow.'

It was 2 am, and Ally was walking to her car in the dark, alone, holding her breath while being aware of what is on the news about missing women.

Ally tried to walk fast without running and heard crackling behind her. She sped up and couldn't resist looking back but didn't see anyone. Catching her breath, she slowed down. She was 5 metres from her car when she heard a car beep in the carpark she was in. Ally saw the lights flash on a car a row over, but saw no one there. Ally felt scared and ran to her car, locked it, and drove home.

The next day Ally checked in with Ivy who was feeling better. Ivy said, 'I only had a 24hr bug, and I will be back at work tonight.'

Ally told Ivy of her experience in the carpark last night and they both thought it was scary. Ivy said, 'We will ask security to walk us to the car from now on.'

'No, we will be fine. It was probably my imagination.' Ally replied.

Ally and Ivy both went to work. All was well, a bit quiet, so they left work early and decided to go to a café and have a coffee before heading home.

When they arrived at the café, they sat in a booth facing the tv in the corner of the café to see what had happened in the news that day. Breaking News came across the screen again.

'Hell,' Ivy said. 'I cannot believe what I am watching.'

'Neither can I,' Ally agreed.

Another body had been found at Mount Macedon. The girl was in her early 20's, same as the other girl, Kia. Fingertips cut off, no teeth, raped and found with no clothes.

Ally said, 'Obviously, a serial killer is out there and no woman is safe.' The police were warning women to lock their homes up at night and not to be in the streets alone at night.

Ally and Ivy's food and coffee came, and the waitress asked if they wanted some magazines to look at while chatting. They both said yes, and the waitress picked some up from the other table and placed them on theirs.

Ally lifted the top magazine and gave it to Ivy, before looking down at the next magazine. It happened to be a wedding book. Ally started to snicker and flicked through the book, about 10 pages in ally saw a picture of Ava and Jax taken in the gardens on their wedding day.

'Ivy look at this. It's is Ava and Jax in a wedding magazine! Why wouldn't she have told us about this, I wonder?' Ally asked. Ivy and Ally where baffled and wondered if they should contact Ava about this but decided to leave it till they got home in a days' time.

Saturday came and Ava and Jax came home from their honeymoon. They invited Ally, Ivy, Blade and Tate over for dinner and to look at their photos. Ava's doorbell rang and it was all her guests arriving at the same time for dinner. They were talking and laughing, sitting with wine and beers looking at pictures from the honeymoon. It was was delightful for all to see. Out of nowhere Ava asked if any more women had been murdered.

'Yes,' Ivy replied. 'It was on the news a day ago. She was found raped with no fingertips or teeth in the same area.'

Ava went white as a ghost! 'Why is this happening? Why hasn't the police caught the killer?' she asked.

No one had answers. During the night Ally asked Ava, 'Why didn't you tell us you were going to put your picture in a wedding magazine?'

'Pardon?' Ava said in disbelief.

'One of your wedding pictures is in a wedding magazine. Why didn't you tell us?' Ally repeated.

'I have no idea what you are talking about, are you sure it is us?' Ava demanded.

'Yes!' Ivy said, deciding to quickly go to the corner store to go buy the book and bring it back. They all had a look and sure enough it was one of their wedding photos.

They couldn't believe what they were seeing, not sure how this happened and who sent it to the magazine. The following Monday Ava rang the magazine and they had no answers other then that someone had it sent to them and liked the picture, so they put it to print in the edition. Sitting dumbfounded there was nothing Ava felt she could do about it.

A CITY IN FEAR

MONTHS AND WEEKS WENT by, more women went missing and more women were found murdered. The women of the city of Melbourne were living in fear. Single mums, shift workers, people out on the town,

Even women that were married, homeless women, all types of women were concerned now. They watched where they went, when, who with; and looked behind them carrying pepper spray or whatever they could get their hands on just to feel some sort of security.

The police over the next few months kept receiving missing persons reports and were under pressure from the public to catch the killer.

One victim was found tied to a tree with ties around her neck and waist, raped and her feet were cut off, another found hanging from a tree with her tongue cut out, another found in a ditch covered in leaves with her breasts cut off. No evidence was found at any of the crime scenes. A professional killer was on the loose and he was trophy collecting from his victims.

People knew about it, the police knew about it and soon the world knew about it. It was sickening, disturbing and surreal all at the same time. Ava and Jax arrived home from a day out, and she started cooking dinner straight away. The doorbell rang so Jax went to the door. He found flowers placed there with no one in sight, he looked around walked to the end of his driveway but found no one.

He brought the flowers inside and showed Ava, 'there was no note, who would they be from?'

'No, not again,' she complained. 'What do you mean?' he asked.

'I received a bunch on our wedding day other than yours and there was no note, but I forgot to tell you. I forgot until now.'

The next day Jax rang the florist using their business name on the packaging and asked who sent flowers to their address.

The florist said, 'I don't know but I remember the person was in a suit with the initials RB on the chest of his suit. Whether that means anything or not I don't know. He was tall, short back and sides, clean shaven, well-groomed and smelt good. That's all I remember, sorry.'

Jax explained all this to Ava and together they both could not work out who this person may be. They went to the police to report it as it had happened twice now, but they said there was nothing they could do.

*   *   *

11 PM THAT NIGHT Ally was awoken abruptly by a strange sound outside. It was a rustling sound in the fallen leaves outside on the grass but peering out the window she couldn't see anything or anyone.

She decided to go outside with a torch to look around her house and still nothing but a little wind. Ally went back to bed. It must have been about a half an hour before Ally jolted back up, there was a tapping on her bedroom window which startled her. This time instead of going to check outside Ally rang Ava and told her she was freaking out with hearing disturbing noises around the house. She was afraid. Jax said he was going to call Tate to come over and stay with her, but in the meantime, she should call the police. The police arrived and checked out Ally's house outside only to find nothing. The took notes and went on their way. Tate turned up just as they were leaving, and stayed the night.

Tate decided to stay with Ally for the week to make her feel safe, but during that week something sparked between them and they started dating. Ally felt safe and happy at long last and was hoping her fairy-tale with Tate would last long term. Ally and Ava checked in with Ivy to make sure she was not feeling threatened in any way, and she said she was fine.

*   *   *

AVA, ALLY, AND IVY all decided to plan a getaway with Jax, Tate and Blade to get away from all the stress of the news and have a break from life in nature. They all packed and headed to Lake Eildon. Packing tents, swags, and canoes they headed off on their road trip following each other.

Ivy drove in the car with Blade and she didn't know him all that well but had met several times on outing's since they have the same friends group so she thought why not go with him on the road trip. Music was playing they were both singing along, laughing at each other singing the wrong words.

'Do you like your work?' Blade asked.

'It pays the bills and I'm saving for a house and a career in law, but I can't afford the life I want if I was to work in a 9-5 job,' she replied.

'Fair enough,' he said. 'That is great that you have goals to work towards.' In getting to know each other, Ivy discovered that Blade was also in law and that they many common interests, including camping, dinning out, movies, day trips, the same taste in music and bands. They hit it off so well that at the next fuel stop Blade went into the store and bought Ivy a drink and snacks for the rest of the trip. Ivy was surprised and feeling girlish, she liked him. So when Blade gave her the food, she kissed him and he returned the kiss. They both smiled, got back in the car and decided to give it a go and stay in the same swag on the weekend away.

*   *   *

THEY ARRIVED AND SET up camp, cracked some beers and wine. They sat and had laughs, drinks and played some games. It was getting hot and steamy, so they all went for a swim and had some fun in the water. They decided to leave canoeing for another day.

The following day was a nice day, light winds but still warm. They all decided to go on a hike through the mountains to the waterfalls and lookouts so they could look down on the town from the mountain tops.

They sang songs on their hike, having fun and feeling good about themselves now that they were all coupled up and all got along so well with each other. Stopping for a water break to catch their breath as the mountain was steep and they were sweating profusely. Taking in the sounds of the forest and breathing in the fresh air they felt relaxed with no tension or worries about a killer on the loose.

Over the next few days they all canoed, fished, swam, got drunk and did nothing but relax in the good company of each other. The time came for them to pack up and drive back home, and they arrived around lunch time feeling refreshed. They all went to Ava's house for a cuppa before they were supposed to go their own ways.

Ava opened the front door and screamed. They all went in the house and saw it was destroyed – they had been robbed. Jax called the police and they came over to the house. When they walked in the door Ava, Ally and Ivy just looked at the police in amazement, standing frozen, as they realised Rise had just walked through the door to assist them in getting details about the robbery. The girl's partners did not know about Rise, as Ivy and Ally were single and didn't have to tell anyone, and Ava hadn't thought twice about him, so she hadn't told Jax.

Jax explained they had gone away for several days and they just got home 20 minutes ago. Rise and his partner called in other police to dust the house to see if any finger prints would show, but to no avail. There was not one ounce of evidence in the house. Rise made a statement that this was done professionally, but they would follow through with an investigation.

Ava fixed up the house a little, put the kettle on and tried to process what had happened, and the others all went home to see if their homes were okay.

Switching the TV on while making a cuppa, low and behold a mid-day movie was on but it paused for another BREAKING NEWS story. Another body had been found in the same location by campers who had called the police to come to the crime scene.

Another young girl mid 20's found bound, raped, gagged and scalped. With each girl they found, the horror of how they died was becoming increasingly violent. How many more victims would there be was the question on everybody's lips. Police held a TV interview addressing the public to be cautious in their daily and night life, warning them not to be alone and always let someone know where they are going, double-check the doors at night, along with windows – check everything.

'We don't want the public to panic, but be vigilant. The perpetrator is not leaving behind any evidence and is very professional at what he is doing. We can confirm there is a serial killer out there and we are doing our very best with what we have to move forward in the investigation. From the bodies that we have found it has been confirmed these young ladies are ladies of the night and work in the adult industry. It seems the killer has a target, but that's not say all women are safe. Still be alert…' the report trailed off.

"Blow me away,' said Ava. 'This has gone for months and no one knew how serious this was and we won't know how may women are missing until someone turns up murdered.'

Ava asked all her friends to come back to her house for dinner after they had gone home to check their homes and unpacked.

They all arrived at Ava and Jax's house and all decided to do a pizza night with light drinks. They had a discussion about the killer is targeting adult workers, and the girls were panicking as the guys couldn't be there to protect them when they left work. So they made a promise to all leave together after work. Then they started thinking about who could be so professional so as not to leave evidence?

Ivy said, 'Police know what they are doing, so does anyone that is involved with the law, or army men.'

Ally called the girls into the kitchen and said, 'What about that copper, Rise? He's creepy and seems to be everywhere we are. And the way he stares at women is not right.'

The girls thought this to be true about Rise, but they thought that it wouldn't be someone they had met as it would be too unbelievable. Plus a police officer? Ivy confirmed, 'there was such a thing as a corrupt police officer, Ally.' Ivy, Ally, and Ava all looked at each other and said, 'No, we are being ridiculous. We're letting the fear, and silly thoughts into our heads.'

*　　*　　*

THE FOLLOWING MONTH EVERYTHING went quite on the murdered women, you could see the public was less nervous going about their life, and people started going out again. Although they were still weary, but no one decided to stop living.

The girls work had gone quiet for period there, but it was starting to pick up again, slowly. Ivy, Ava, and Ally met at work and they were excited to go back as they were running out of money and bills kept coming in. The night started slow but increased with customers and after 10pm it became quite busy. The strange thing was how Ivy, Ava, Ally were paranoid and were looking at all the customers with caution and suspicion. They couldn't seem to relax to do their job and it became obvious that the serial killer had psychologically taken an effect on the girls. The shift ended and they all walked to their cars together and none of them left until they could all see each other locked in their cars, then they would all go home.

Jax was asleep when Ava got home so she snuck into bed and kissed him good night.

Ivy got home and Blade was watching movies because he couldn't sleep, so he stayed up and waited for her to get home, then they went off to bed together.

Ally got home and it seemed dark, even though it was 2am Tate always left a little night light on for her to see coming into the house. Ally got out of the car, opened the front door and called for Tate but there was no answer. Ally walked around the house, checked the bed and no sign of him. No note was left, she thought he may just have gone out with his mates and got too drunk to drive home, so she went to bed.

The following day Tate came home around lunch time. Ally asked, 'Did you have a big night on the town?'

'No,' he replied. 'My mate Jack asked me to go shooting with him, so I took up the offer, and stayed at his cabin for the night as it was too far to come home.'

'Oh,' said Ally. 'Is your work ok with you not going in last night?'

'Yeah, they were okay.' Tate worked at the newspaper printing warehouse, as far as Ally knew.

And with all the murders over the last few months they had been busy with print, but he informed Ally since it is been slowing down, he took the night off.

Rise made a phone call to Ava to tell her that the investigation on their robbery was now a closed case. No evidence was found, and they have no leads.

Ivy, Ally and Ava decided to go to the local RSL for dinner before work and all met at 6pm. They placed their orders and had a glass of Rose Moscato each.

The 6pm news came on the TV up on the wall hanging in the corner, a male's body had been found 1km away from where the women's bodies had been discovered over the last several months. Caucasian male, 22 year's old, was found raped and tortured whilst alive, then strangled to death.

The RSL went silent instantly, all the people were just looking at each other and shaking their heads. Police were saying they don't think it was related to the serial killer but would still follow all leads and update the public as soon as they could.

The girls finished dinner and went on to work. The most recent news broadcast was the talk of the night in the dressing rooms.

At work it was another productive night and they made more than usual, although it did not seem busier than any other night. Time flew, and it was time for them to have a break. Ally checked her phone and saw she had a missed call from her mum. She rang her mum back and found out that she was in hospital – she had a heart attack. Ally said, 'Mum, I'm leaving work right now and I'm coming to the hospital to see you and will stay at your house for the night.'

Ivy and Ava heard the conversation and said, 'Just go. We'll tell Joe, I'm sure he won't mind as this is serious.'

Ally hugged Ava and Ivy, and said 'I'll call you tomorrow to update you on mum, I may have to stay down there longer, I will go with the flow. Love you guys.'

Ava and Ivy went back to work while Ally changed into her normal clothes, grabbed her handbag and went to her car without a second thought. She was on her own and it wasn't until she got home she realised she was alone.

Tate was not home and Ally thought he was at work, so she left him a note.

Dear Tate,

I was at work and had a missed phone call from mum, I've left work to go to the hospital. Mum has had a heart attack and I don't know how long I will be staying with mum for, but I will contact you in the coming days to let you know what's happening.

Love you Tate with all my heart. Speak soon.
Love Ally.

Tate arrived home to Ivy's letter and called her, 'Is your mum ok?'

'Yeah, she's okay. Weak, and confused, but she will be okay. I am coming home tomorrow about 5 pm, will you be home?' she asked.

'Yes,' he said. 'See you then.'

Friday came around and Ivy came home to Tate. He was waiting with open arms.

'Sorry I missed you, Tate, but I had to leave at once,' she explained. 'It's okay, Ivy,' he said comforting her. 'Let's call the others to catch up tonight for drinks.'

Everyone gathered at the local pub for drinks and a Friday night catch up. Tate was telling everyone about his shooting trip he went on the other night and that his friend said they could all go to his cabin in the woods for a holiday away for a week or so if they wanted to.

'What do you think, guys?' he asked. 'It is a beautiful place in the forest at Woodend.'

All agreed to take more time off work, and decided to take a week away at Tate's friend's cabin. They decided to leave next Friday and return the following Friday.

NO NEWS IS GOOD NEWS

ALL THROUGHOUT THE WORKING week they were calling each other with excitement about going away. The guys had their gun license, so they were excited to go shooting and fishing as well.

Thursday night came, the girls finished work early at 1am, and all walked to their cars with excitement to go home and pack. As they were walking to their cars they could see lights flashing down the road, road blocks and they wondered what happened.

Ally said, 'Let's go over and see what is going on.' Holding each other's hands, they crossed the road and walked down a block to where they saw all the commotion. Suddenly crowds started appearing and they squished their way to the front of the road block barrier which was in front of an alley way. Five or so dumpsters were down there and the police had brought down lighting that lit up the alley way.

A blonde woman was laying on the ground naked and bloodied. The girls took a breath in, and couldn't believe what they saw. It was close to home, close to work. All the other victims had been found in the forest now one in an alley way?

Ava asked, 'Is this connected to the serial killer murders. Why in the city?' Ivy commented, 'I am glad we are going away.'

Ally called over a police officer who, to their surprise when he turned around, turned out to be Rise. Rise walked towards the girls and their stunned faces.

'Hey, Rise, what has happened?' Ally asked.

'Another murder. Looks like this girl worked in an adult club as well, by the look of her clothes which were torn off. We must do testing to find out who she is, it will be broadcasting on the morning news.'

'Is she decapitated like the others?' Ally asked.

'Do not repeat what I tell you,' said Rise. 'But yes. She has had her tongue cut out, her privates slashed, raped, and strangled. What a horrible way to go.'

'Thank Rise, that was in depth,' Ivy replied. Rise asked what they were doing for the weekend, out of general chit chat.

Ivy said, 'We are going to Woodend for a week.'

'Nice,' he replied. 'I'm up that way actually this weekend for some time out, looking at these bodies has some effect on you physically. Sometimes you need a break, before you break.'

They girls nodded and said, 'Yes, I don't know how you do it.'

Ally, Ivy, Ava said good-bye and walked back to their cars and headed for home.

After hours of sleep Ally woke up, flicked on the TV and saw the morning news was on.

'The victim found last night in the alley way was Angel Montana, aged 21. She lived locally and worked at Hire A Lady Escort Service. It seems the crime is linked to the serial killer, as we investigate further, we hope to find some evidence. We will keep the public updated, in the meantime please stay safe.'

Ally got on the phone immediately and rang Ava, 'Hey, Ava, it's Ally. I just watched the news and they released the girls name and its Angel Montana, that's your friend isn't it?'

Ava was silent in disbelief. She decided to go to Angel's parents' home to pay her respects.

Ava arrived at the house in Green Tree's estate and knocked on the door, but it seemed quiet. Ava waited five minutes before someone opened the door.

It was Angel's father, Roy. 'Hi, Ava. Please come in.'

Walking into the kitchen, he asked, 'Would you like a cuppa, Ava?'

'Yes please.' Taking a seat at the table Ava looked toward the doorway that lead to the bedrooms and standing there was Angel's mum, Jean. Ava stood up and simply hugged her for what seemed like ten minutes. They cried a little together.

Jean asked, 'how could this happen, Ava, to our Angel?'

'I don't know, Jean. All the girls know not to walk the streets alone, I can't help but wonder why Angel was alone. The only possible answer that comes to mind is that she knew this person and trusted being alone with them. I cannot think of any other reason for her to be alone out there. Jean, may I look through her room?'

'Of course, Ava, and if you choose to keep something please feel free to do so.'

Ava went to the bedroom door and slowly opened it, it was creaking slightly and sounded eerie. With an odd silence, Ava stood in the room and looked around. There were posters of Whitney Houston, Queen, Adele… Angel had various taste in music.

Ava walked over to the bed which was not slept in, Angel must of made it before going to work. She took a seat on the bed and just sat. Angel give me some clues to help you, help me find your killer Angel.

Angel's bedroom window was open slightly and a breeze came through with a white butterfly that landed on Angel's dressing table.

Coincidental or not, Ava walked over to the dresser. The butterfly had landed on a book, and Ava picked up the book and had a look. It was a diary that Angel kept. She decided to keep it and take it home, since the police had not taken it for evidence.

'Thanks Jean and Roy, for letting me come to see you both. I am going to keep her diary if that is okay? Please send me the details of the funeral, so I can attend.'

Ava got home and called the girls to come over. When they arrived Ava told them she had got hold of Angel's dairy in the hope there were any clues in there.

They flicked through page after page of stories about her girlfriends at work, what kind of money she made nightly. She talked about how her Instagram was getting more and more attention, and she was becoming more popular on social media. She even talks about girl's night outs.

Ivy said, 'There's nothing really in here, Ava. But we'll keep reading, I want to be sure.'

Three-quarter's of the way into the diary, on a new page:

I meet this amazing man.

Ally said, 'Okay, let's keep reading and see what this man's about.'

Dear Diary

I met this man today at work.

Saw him come in a couple of times over the last month. I thought it was because he was new to the place, he liked it and kept coming back. I had given him a couple of dances, he tips well, but once I had left him, he didn't cross my mind again.

He officially approached me on my break and introduced himself, as did I. We talked and he said he was new in town, that he moved here due to work, and worked for the government.

'Ava did angel tell you about this man?' asked Ivy.

'No, she didn't, she wanted to see how far it would go with him before she told anyone, I think.'

'Turn the page,' Ivy said. 'Wait, let's get a glass of wine each.'

Ally went into the kitchen and poured them all a glass of wine and then sat to continue to read the diary.

Dear Diary

I went on out to lunch at Apple bee's café for a date. The day was stunning, the sun was out with a warm breeze, birds chirping, people on their phones were passing by, and music playing in the cars as they drove by.

I ordered a chicken caesar salad and he ordered a steak with veggies; he had a beer and I had a white wine. We talked a bit and got to know each other a little. He told me he was working for the government but could not confirm his duties, due to confidentiality or tell me what he did. I accepted that. It was just nice that a man was genuinely interested in me, I have trouble dating due to the work I do. Men do not understand that it is just my job – it does not define who I am as a person.

He buys me flowers, gifts, showers me with affection. It's nice and I am starting to like him more than I care to admit.

'She hasn't signed his name anywhere girls, why? So, we know she met a new man who works in government and treats her well. Let's keep reading,' Ivy said.

Dear Diary

Had my first sleepover with my new man. We have been dating 2 months now, so I felt comfortable enough to sleep with him.

His apartment was clinical and clean, which I thought unusual but he always said he like's cleanliness in his home.

Make yourself feel at home go tour my home if you like, he said to me. It took me about 20 minutes to look around. It was a double-, story large house; I could see he made an extraordinary amount of money from how he lived.

Started at the top and worked my way down. There was a door I tried to open but it had a padlock on it. Why is this door padlocked, work stuff he replied?

Night-time came and we did the deed, but throughout the night he was requesting unusual gratification – strange positionings, that I was not comfortable with.

We continued with what he wanted, but the times after that I refused. It felt creepy and I said no, we can make love like normal people.

Just after I said it I noticed he got slightly aggressive and angry, I was a bit scared. I only slept there three more times after that. He said sorry but I could see his frustration in the bedroom.

Dear Diary

I decided to stop dating with the Man. I thought was a gentleman, but I am finding myself feeling uncomfortable with him increasingly.

I am getting ready to go to work tonight, but before I leave I just want to ring mum and dad to say hello as I normally do, and then I rang him to end things. Voicemail came on and I left him a message ending things and off to work I went.

Work was busy last night chocka-block full of appointments, one after the other. Back at our work building we have a lounge for customers to lounge and have a drink and meet the girls. After I finished my appointments I stayed back for a while. There where so many men there as it was a long weekend. Got a drink and sat on the lounge just to rest and people watch.

As I was looking through the crowd, I saw a man that looked familiar. I went up behind him at the bar and tapped him on the shoulder, he turned around and it was him.

OMG.

DID HE NOT GET MY MESSAGE?

What are you doing here, did you not get my message, I asked?

No, he said I have been working and thought I would wait here and surprise you when you got back.

My heart was racing and my hands started to sweat. I felt sick in the stomach, I felt awkward, how do I deal with this? I signalled to the bartender to get me a drink.

Umm, I said, this is awkward, but I have left you a message on your phone, I think we should end things; I just do not think it is going to go anywhere.

His face instantly changed, his pupils went black and he was furious, I could tell. He said nothing, finished his drink gave me an evil stare and left without a word.

'That's it,' Ally yelled. 'She did not sign his name in her diary for sure he has to be her killer; what do you think girls?'

'It sounds like he has motive but there is nothing detailing who he is, we are at a dead end. I think we should take it to the police regardless,' Ivy replied. Off they went to the police station and handed in the diary of Angel Montana to the officer at the desk, but not before photocopying it all.

The police took it and said they would read it.

The girls gathered with the guys and told them about Angel's diary and the man she wrote about in it. The boys agreed it gave this man motive to kill, but Tate said, 'He did not know her that long, so he probably just walked away.'

Ivy said, 'I guess we'll never know. There is no name or picture of him, no DNA found on her. But we know he worked in government if we know nothing else.'

'I feel useless,' said Ava.

She loved life, had a great heart, went out of her way to help people in need, she did not deserve this, and I am sure the other girls did not either.

While everybody was sitting together, Jean, Angel's mum rang and informed Ava that the funeral would be on Friday.

'We will be there, Jean, see you then.' Ava replied.

The funeral was at St Mary's a big old grand blue stone church at Milena, it was over 100 years old. People gathered from everywhere; Ava, Ivy and Ally with the guys turned up in support of Ava losing her friend.

The ceremony started; the coffin was on the trolley draped in the most gorgeous flowers you had ever seen. It was Angel's favourite flowers gerberas and iris with green foliage.

On a stand next to the coffin was a large portrait of Angel. She had a beautiful smile and was holding her cat Smokey, a Russian Blue she loved so much.

Tears flowed as the family was making speeches and revisiting memories and good times they shared with Angel. Angel's mum Jean wanted everyone to celebrate the life she had rather than her death.

THREE BECOMES TWO

Aｆter the funeral on Friday, they went on their week away incredibly early Saturday morning. They all packed and all met at Jax and Ava's house at 5.30am to begin their road trip.

It was still dark, the sun hadn't risen yet and the air was cool. All the cars were packed and lined up in front of Ava's. They all got in their cars, put their headlights and radio on, and followed each other down the highway to their location in the woods. The sun came up and it was a beautiful mix orange and pink colours lighting up the morning sky.

Ivy rang the others and said, 'Let's stop at the next food place for breakfast.'

'Okay,' they all replied. Down the highway there was a super large truckie stop with freshly cooked meals to offer.

They all got out of the cars and walked into restaurant part of the servo, and ordered bacon and eggs with coffee's for breakfast. As they sat waiting for their meals, they were discussing Angel's death and hoping the killer has been captured, talking about how Angel absolutely knew not to go out onto the streets alone.

Ally said, 'I must believe she knew the person she was with outside her work otherwise I don't believe she would of went out. Did security see her leave with anyone? Was the camera's working when she left, we will have to ask Rise after our week away to see if they have progressed any further in finding the killer.'

Breakfast came and it smelt good. All hungry they ate like they had never eaten before; they did not eat much food at the funeral, so they were hungry for food and coffee.

Buying extra snacks for the road trip, off they headed, all laughing and happy to put the miserable news behind them of what is going on in the city.

An hour went by and Ivy messaged Jax to say she needed a toilet stop. They were approaching dirt roads towards the forest, so Jax replied with "we will drive into the forest Ivy as there is no more toilet stops until we get to the cabin."

Driving deep into the forest they found a campground with a public toilet. They all turned off their cars, stretched and had a toilet break.

Tate said 'Why don't we came here tonight and have a little adventure, we can sleep in our cars. It won't hurt for one night.

Ava, Ally and Ivy all replied in excitement, 'Yes, let's do that.'

'Okay, it's decided then.'

They smelt the fresh air in the forest, the eucalyptus smells from the gumtrees, heard the bees around the wattles, and just the smell of fresh grass and air. Ally stood with her arms spread far apart spinning around with joy.

'Shhhh… listen,' said Ivy. 'Kookaburra's, they sound so beautiful.'

Blade, Tate and Jax went off into the woods to collect wood for a night fire. They had only snacks on them, as Ally and the girls were going to do shopping when they got to the cabin. The girls decided while the guys were out wood hunting that they would follow a track they saw not far away, so off they went happily through the forest.

Twenty minutes into their walk they saw a sign, Reef's Waterfall Lookout this way.

They all looked at each other in agreeance to see the waterfall. They travelled down steep terrain, with ferns lining the tracks creating a rainforest feel. There were natural smells, birds chirping, and they were so relaxed. From off in the far distance they heard the waterfall rushing and clashing on the rocks.

Coming up on a sign 900 metres to Waterfall another sign, Shortcut. 'Let's take the short cut,' said Ivy. 'As we will need to get back to camp soon — we didn't leave the guys a note.'

They went down the track of the shortcut but after ten mins Ava said, 'I cannot hear the waterfall anymore.' Standing still they all tried to hear the waterfall, but nothing.

'Shush,' Ally said. 'Did you hear that?'

'No. What?' the other girls asked. 'Crackling in the bushes.'

'No, wait yes, I just heard it,' said Ava. 'It's getting closer, lets run forget the waterfall.' They started running in a panic through scrub and trees as fast as they could, not taking notice of their direction. Ava tripped over a log and both Ally and Ivy stopped to help her up. They looked around and said, 'Where are we? OH MY GOD, ARE WE LOST?'

Ally was crying uncontrollably so Ava wrapped her arms around her.

'Ally, we will work it out. We have a little bit of daylight left. They couldn't hear the waterfall and didn't recognise the surroundings they stood in. Ava, the positive one out of them, said, 'Okay, let us walk this way.'

They walked for thirty minutes in the hope of finding their way out for the night, but in the distance Ivy heard a chopping sound. She listened to the direction it was coming from, and said, 'To our left. Let's go.'

Sunset was coming up and they saw a farmhouse where they heard the chopping coming from.

As they approached the house they yelled out, 'HELLO! Is anybody there?' Blade, Tate, and Jax got back to camp to find nobody there.

'Where are the girls?' asked Blade.

Jax replied, 'They probably just went out for a walk down that track over there exploring. I wouldn't think they would be long, let's start the fire for them.' The heat from the crackling fire was warming and cosy, they all cracked a beer and chatted amongst each other.

The sun had just gone down, and they started to worry.

'Let's go down the track a little and call out to them,' suggested Blade. Walking down the track with torches and calling out, they got no response. 'My God, where are they, where could they be?'

'If they're playing a joke, it's not a good one,' complained Tate. Away from the fire they felt the chill in the air getting colder and colder, even though the day had been nice.

Going back to camp they were very worried. They all sat in Jax's car to decide what to do.

Blade said, 'It looks like they're lost and they would be so scared, but we can't see in the dark and I think Ava is smart enough to keep them safe for the night. In the morning we will go again to search.'

*　　*　　*

FROM THE BACK OF the farmhouse a dirty, toothless older man popped out to see what the yelling was about. At the front of his house he saw three girls who looked cold and lost. As the girls got closer to the house, they saw it was an old, worn, and rickety house that had been there for centuries.

When they looked at the man, they were not sure if they were relieved or frightened.

Wearing a flannelette shirt under overall with an apron full of blood. The girls froze as he said, 'Can I help you girls?'

Ivy and ally could not find words to speak.

'Hello,' Ava said. 'We are lost and can't find our way back to camp, we took a wrong turn somewhere and now we are lost. We are camping over the night before moving on tomorrow. Would you mind if we could use your phone please?'

'I am Joe, by the way. Your welcome to come inside, my wife is in there, but we don't have a phone, sorry. Come inside, it's very cold out her for you ladies.' Hesitant but cold they slowly walked to the house afraid, and the smell from Joe was so strong it was making them ill.

'Hey Ma,' yelled Joe. 'Boil the water, we have company.'

'All right, Pa!'

The house was run down with white paint peeling off from decades of being in the weather and cobwebs hanging off the windows. They were so dirty you could barely see through them. Opening the front door, it creaked so loud it gave them chills. They walked up the hall behind Joe into the kitchen, the walls were filthy, the floorboards squeaking as they walked down the hall.

Upon entering the kitchen, Joe's wife welcomed us.

'Hello young lady's, I will make you all a hot cuppa coffee.' All the girls said thank you, as they took a seat on the dirty dining room chairs. They looked around the room which seemed so dusty and looked like it had not been cleaned ever.

Joe said to the girls, 'We have rooms out in the backyard. You can stay out there the night, but do not wonder around, in the morning I'll drive you to a main road.'

Ivy, Ally and Ava all looked at each other and nodded, they were scared but didn't have a choice really as it was dark and cold outside.

'Goodnight,' Joe's wife said as they followed Joe out to the backyard. He lived on thirty acres and there were a lot of different sheds, old cars and machines on the property. The night was eerie and windy, Joe opened the door to what looked like a really large type of caravan.

They got in and said, 'Thanks so much Joe, we really are grateful. 'Sleep tight,' said Joe.

Ava shut the door behind Joe, looked at the others and they all felt like they could breath for the first time in hours. They laid on the beds chatting about the bloody night from hell that they had.

Ivy said, 'The boys are going to be so worried not knowing what's happened to us. We can't ring them, we can't let them know at all what's happened. Let's hope they do a search for us in the morning.'

They all fell asleep; they were so exhausted.

Ava heard shuffling noises at around 3am in the morning. She was scared to roll over and look around, but she did slowly.

'Ally what are you doing awake?'

'Go back to sleep I am just going outside to go the toilet. I think that coffee made me ill, I feel sick.'

'Okay,' said Ava, and rolled back over to go to sleep.

Ally grabbed the torch and walked a little bit away from the caravan near an old, rusty gutted-out car. Squatting under the moonlight to pee, Ally pulled up her pants when she heard something behind her. As she looked around there was a thud, she was out cold.

Ava and Ivy sat up in their beds to look at each other. 'Where is Ally, Ava?' Ivy asked.

Ava replied, 'I don't know, she woke me up early this morning and told me she was going to the toilet. I rolled over and went back to sleep so I didn't see if she returned to bed. Maybe she is at the house having coffee, we should get dressed and go to the house.'

Opening the door of the caravan they felt the fresh morning breeze. The sun was shining but the fresh morning air made the girls cold and shiver a little. Holding hands, they made their way through the long grass on the land and dodged many old cars. They could see smoke coming out of the chimney so they knew they were awake.

Knocking on the door, Joe opened and said, 'Come in. The kettle is hot for coffee, where is the other girl there was three of you last night?'

Ava said, 'We thought she must have been here having coffee as she was not in the van when we woke up.'

'No,' Joe replied. 'I have been up since 5am and nobody has been here. Ma, have you seen the girl?'

'No.'

Ava and Ivy's face went white, feeling sick to the stomach, Ivy said, 'She would not have just taken off, Ava. That is just not like her.'

'I know, I know I can't think now. I don't know what to think now, we were going to take off together to find camp and now we need to find Ally.'

Joe suggested they take a walk around the land down to the creek that lies at the back of the property and call her name. He would check on his buggy the other parts of the property and call out for her there.

'ALLY! ALLY! ALLY WHERE ARE YOU!' both girls called out.

No response, so they went down to the creek and could hear the rushing water. They made their way to the water's edge, looking down in both directions but they found and heard nothing.

Walking back up the hill back to the property, they continued to call out.

*　*　*

WEARILY RUBBING HER EYES, Ally woke up with a sore head. Ally noticed that she was gagged and handcuffed to a pole, trapped in what looked like a underground cave of some sort. Shivering from the morning chill, she couldn't warm up as when she went to the toilet last night she only had her shirt and shorts on with no jumper. She looked around in absolute fear. She had no idea where she was or why. The last thing Ally recalled was going to the toilet.

From afar, Ally could hear her name being yelled out but it was so distant she knew it must be Ivy and Ava looking for her. But she knew that calling out more than likely would not be heard, but she tried anyway, even with her mouth gagged. Joe, Ava, and Ivy all met at the house defeated. Joe went into the house, while Ava and Ivy spoke privately.

Ava said to Ivy, 'Okay, our plan is to leave here. We will get Joe to take us back to camp since he said he thinks he knows where our site is. We will meet with the guys, hoping that they haven't left, tell them what's happened, and we shall call the police to come and search.'

'Sounds like a plan,' said Ivy.

Joe warmed up his old farming ute and the girls jumped in. Joe knows the area well and the overnight stops that people camp at, so he went to a couple and the girls said no they're not it. He stopped at the next one and they saw the guys waving.

'Yes, Joe, that's it. They're our boyfriends, thank you for bringing us here. We are going to call the police to come back up to search the area, so you may get them knocking at your door asking you questions.'

Joe left and the guys looked at the girl's pale faces.

'So happy to see you, what happened, we have been worried sick? WHERE IS ALLY?' Tate screamed.

'Okay guys, this is what happened. We walked the track over there till we came to waterfall signs and there was a sign saying there was a short cut so we took it because it was getting late but before we knew it we didn't make it the waterfall and we realised we were lost. We kept walking till sunset and came across an old farmhouse and the people there let us stay the night in a caravan, the three of us. Around 3am Ally went out to go to the toilet and when we woke this morning she was not there, and we did a small search and calling out to her but nothing,' explained Ava. 'Guys we need to go the police straight away.'

Packing up, they headed into town. Arriving at the police station Ava spoke and told them what had happened.

The officer said, 'Take a seat and I'll get someone to take you into a room and get all the details so we can begin a search, Ava.'

A door opened to an office off the side of the waiting room, and both Ava and Ivy were called in. Low and behold it was Rise, greeted by Ava and Ivy's face. They all just stared at each other.

'Rise, what are you doing up here?' Ivy asked.

'I work where I am needed from week to week. I don't work at one station, regional or local throughout the state.' The girls were finding it hard to believe that wherever they were Rise happened to be there, but he was a police officer so not knowing their schedule or how they work they shrugged it off.

'Okay,' Rise said. 'Tell your story from the start, Ava.'

Ava told the story from start to end; Rise told them that they all may want to get a motel for a couple of days while they try to find Ally. Rise organised a search party, the locals got hold of what happened and wanted to join in search. The media found out and published a piece, sniffer dogs were following tracks and at least 80 people were searching by this point. Rise knocked on Joe's door and interviewed Joe about his side of the story, and Rise asked if it would be okay to search. And search they did, but they found nothing down the creek or on Joe's land. It was a big space of land to search, but no evidence was found. Rise left the house to join the other searchers in the forest for the next five hours, but nothing. The search finished, because it was getting dark, but would continue tomorrow.

*   *   *

JOE WENT TO WHERE Ally was, and the fear on her face was clear.

'Don't scream, lovely one, or the pain will get worse.' Joe took Ally's pants off, tied her legs apart and inserted his penis. Ally was crying, and tried to shake her head for him to stop, but he didn't. He smelt dirty while he raped her.

When he finished, he laughed and left her with her pants off. He bought over a table and tied her to it to torture her.

Ally was begging for her life but Joe ignored her. Joe started ripping off her finger and toenails one by one, then he sliced the back of her ankles so she couldn't run out.

Joe said, 'I'm sorry you were the one Ally, but you were just in the wrong place at the wrong time.'

Ally cried and moaned, 'You bastard.' She could do nothing. Hours went by and Joe raped her again. Then he inserted a drill into her vagina and turned it on, blood flew everywhere and Ally passed out.

He then went on to stitch up her vagina then he left her there. He came back an hour later.

Blasting the radio and singing tunes to himself, he cut open her shirt and cut off her nipples. Ally awoke with a jolt of pain. Trying to get him to stop, tears were streaming down her face. She felt weak with blood loss and tied helplessly she knew this was the end for her.

Joe sliced Ally's throat and cut off her hands. Joe seemed pleased with himself. Blood was everywhere. He wrapped up Ally's body, carried it to his mincer and disposed of her body completely.

When he went back into his house his wife said, 'You've had your fun now. Go shower and I will make you something to eat.'

The next morning, Rise arrived at Joe's to see if Ally may have turned up there.

'No, I have not seen her, sir. Do you have a card in case she does turn up?' Rise handed him his card and went on his way.

Joe's house was hidden; the two closest houses were five kilometres away in another direction. The search members became bigger by morning, there was 150 to help search the tracks and forest around the national park.

Helping in the search of course was Blade, Jax, Tate, Ava and Ivy. They were looking, but horrified when thinking what may have happened to her, no one had an explanation.

Five days went past, and no evidence or information was produced to the police. They didn't want the FBI to get on the case, but by the next morning, they all turned up to take over.

In charge of FBI was Mia Gauci. She introduced herself to Rise and asked, 'Where the friends of this girl Ally were?'

Rise said, 'I will take you to the motel they're staying at.' Mia made her way to her car to follow Rise.

At the motel they were all gathered in Jax and Ava's room. Ivy was crying when they heard a knock on the door. Blade got up to open the door and saw both officers standing there and asked them to come in. Mia told them they were taking over Ally's case and wanted to hear the story from them again.

'From now on,' Mia said. 'You contact me if you remember anything or need updates. Here is my card, we will do our best to find her. You may want to go home or do what you were going to do up this way.'

Blade said, 'We were all going away, but just stopped here over night before we went on. I don't think it's right to holiday in this time of tragedy.'

'You all go home now and if I have any updates, I will contact you, Ava.'

HEADING HOME

HEADING HOME WAS A sorrowful journey filled with disbelief. They had all lost a friend and were not feeling right about heading home without Ally.

Ava's phone had been ringing hot for some time now, but she hadn't had the courage to answer it, knowing it was Ally's mum. Ava decided to answer it when she arrived home, had a hot shower, make a cuppa and had a chance to wrap her head around everything.

Two and a half hours later they all arrived home and went their own ways. Ava did as planned and got into that shower, while Jax put the kettle on and the T.V. It was all over the news and when Ava came out from the shower in her robe and wet hair. She stared at the T.V and broke down crying.

'How could this happen to Ally, Jax?'

'Here, here is your cuppa. Ring Ally's mum.'

Ava dialled the number and there was not even time for a ring before Ally's mum picked up.

Ava could hardly understand her because she was crying so much, 'AVA, AVA what happened to my Ally? Ava it's on the news, that's how I found out. Is she dead, Ava? IS SHE DEAD?' she dissolved into hysterical tears.

'I honestly don't know. She hasn't been found, the circumstances are just so strange. I don't understand it either, we were all together, Pam,' Ava said. 'Pam I am going to come over tomorrow and we will talk about the funeral.'

The next day came and Ava and Jax went over to Pam's house. Shortly after their arrival, Ivy and Blade turned up. Pam was still distraught and collapsed into a heap on the couch crying outrageously. They were trying to decide on whether or not to have a memorial. Pam didn't want to think about is as she still had hope Ally was alive.

At that moment there was another knock at the door, it was Mia from the FBI.

'Hi Pam, I'm Mia from the FBI. I'm looking after your daughter's case. What I can tell you is that it's been a few days now, we are not giving up the search but will have to in the near future. For now we are still searching, we will go back to the farmhouse where they were staying and double- check there again. But I need to tell you that there is no evidence whatsoever. Pam I'm going to be honest with you, I don't think she would be alive. So it looks like your deciding to have a vigil for Ally and I would go ahead with doing that.'

The FBI made the day trip back to Joe's farmhouse with several detectives to do another thorough search of the property, the creek and the nearby national park and dead-end roads. Mia stumbled upon an earring near the van the girls were staying in, she picked it up and bagged it, but told nobody just yet of her discovery.

Staying in town overnight, all the detectives went to the local pub for dinner before they called it a night. Come the next morning Mia knocked on the door of her partner and said, 'John do you have a minute?'

'Yes,' he said.

'I'm going to direct all the detectives to go back to Joe's farmhouse. When I was there today I realised we had not gone through all those sheds he has on the property. The reason I'm saying this is because I found this yesterday, an earring. I'm going to send a picture of it to Ava, Pam and Ivy to see if they can confirm anything. I'm also waiting on a warrant to come through so we can go through everything.'

*   *   *

BING, BING. BING. PAM'S, Ava's and Ivy's phone all went off at the same time.

'This is weird who is sending us a message?' Ivy asked.

They opened their message which said: Hi ladies, does this earing belong to any of you, have you seen it before?

Regards Mia.

Both Pam and Ivy replied with a no. But Ivy replied: yes, I bought them for Ally for her last birthday.

*   *   *

PING. MIA OPENED HER message and saw the two negative answers and one yes from Ivy. Bingo!

'John it's Ally's earring, we had it confirmed by Ivy. Joe's farmhouse is our focus. John, please round up all the detectives for a meeting and I will just quickly go to reception to see if our warrant has come through.'

Mia got to the reception, 'Hi guys has a fax come through for me yet?' Just as she finished her sentence the fax went off and the lady behind the desk said, 'Here you go.'

'Thank you.'

Mia walked back to the carpark where everybody was waiting.

'Right guys we have found evidence so the sole focus is on Joe's farmhouse and all of the sheds on his property. Do not miss ANYTHING! Turnover whatever you need to take samples if you feel you must, take evidence kits with you, leave nothing unturned.'

*　　*　　*

MIA AND HER DETECTIVES turned up at Joe's, she told detectives, 'Stay in the cars until I go to the door to hand over the warrant. I will wave when I have handed over the warrant.'

They knocked at the door, then Mia and John were waited for the door to open. No answer, so they knocked again. While waiting they could hear the cows and the pigs he had on his property down the back end of the acreage.

'Hold your horses I am coming! Hey I heard you,' Joe opened the door. 'Hello again.'

'Hello Joe, we are here to tell you we have a warrant to look through your house and property.'

'Why you have already searched here?'

'We are going to do one more thorough look, here is the warrant.'

'MA GET DRESSED, WE HAVE COMPANY,' he yelled. Mia turned around and signalled the detectives. All at once they all got out the cars with their kits and went into the house and the others scattered on the property. Hours went past and they found nothing in the house. Joe and his wife where interviewed again but they told them nothing new although Joe's wife was extremely quiet. Out on the grounds, there were a least five sheds they had to thoroughly go over. Mia and John checked out the shed closest to the van they stayed in, turning everything upside down – nothing. In one of the sheds a detective saw a hair and bagged it up for evidence, then siz hours into the search a detective yelled to Mia, 'OVER HERE!'

'What is it, what do you have?'

'It's a mincer. A big, heavy industrial mincer that's been cleaned but has some remnants of some sort of blood and meat in it.' Carefully looking closer Mia could see something in the blades. Everyone around them suited up in gloves and carried it to the back of the larger police van, it was to be take back to the lab for forensics to do their magic. Mia went into the house to talk to them and told them what they had taken and told them not to leave town and that they would be hearing from them again.

As Mia slowly walked out the kitchen in through the lounge towards the front door, there was a table with family photo's. Mia stopped to look at them all and proceeded to walk to the door, but then paused in her tracks, walked back to the table and noticed a familiar face. Picking up the frame to hold it closer to her, she was amazed that the familiar face was Tate.

'Joe, can you come in here please?'

Joe walked into the lounge area, 'Oh your looking at the pictures.'

'Yes, can you tell me who this is, Joe?'

'This young boy? Umm, my son.'

'What is his name, Joe?'

'Tate, why? He lives in Melbourne I don't see him much.'

'Okay,' said Mia. 'Joe we will be in touch do not leave town.'

'Ma,' Joe said. 'I used the mincer to dispose of that girl's body and fed her to the pigs, but I washed it good, they won't find anything.'

'Jesus Christ, Joe. what if they do, huh? We are both going to prison and they will think Tate is involved as well.'

Mia, John and the detectives all headed back to Melbourne. Along the way Mia rang Ava and told her to have everybody at her house by 6pm.

Ava rang everyone, gathered them all over and put the kettle on.

'I wonder what this is all about, guys. Maybe they found her or something?' Ava rang Pam and told her to come over as well since it was about her daughter. Making them all a cuppa, she put out biscuits while they waited for Mia to arrive. Running late, Mia turned up 6.30pm.

'Sorry guys I had things to do. Okay, I wanted you all here because I want to update you all every step of the way. I don't want you to be in the dark or hear things through social media. Going back to Joe's house we did an extensive search and what we found of interest was a mincer in one of the sheds and hair. They have been taken to the lab for forensics to do their tests. When I get the results, which should be tomorrow or the next day, I will let you know. The mincer had been washed but we could still see blood and some sort of meat in the blades. I know this sounds horrible, but I want to be honest with you all.' Pam let out a loud cry, and they all stopped to hug her.

'One more thing, Tate, what's your father's name?' they all looked at Tate wondering why she was asking him this.

'Joe,' Tate replied. 'Why?'

'Because the farmhouse where the girls stayed was your mother and father's house.'

'WHAT!' Tate said.

WHAT! echoed Ivy, Jax, Blade and Ava. 'How do you know?' they all asked.

'Saw Tate's picture on the table in the hallway and asked Joe who he was, and he told me.'

'Girls you were at my dad's? Oh my God, I did not think we were near there.'

'Tate, we need you to come down to the station for questioning.'

'What why? Please do not tell me you think I had something to do with Ally's disappearance. Oh my God, I cannot believe this is happening. Guys, you must believe me.'

Mia put Tate into the police car and they drove off. None of them had any words to say, they were in shock. They were all saying, 'No, Tate cannot have anything to do with this.'

'He has not seen his father in over eight years.' Ivy said. She understand that Joe may have killed Ava. Pam was sobbing from the overload of information and the thought that her daughter may have been put through a mincer and fed to pigs. It was something incomprehensible. Jax drove Pam home and made sure she went to bed safely before driving back home.

At the station Tate sat in a cold barely-lit room. Tate watched Mia walk through the door and took a seat.

'Tate, this conversation will be recorded. The time is 8pm on April 11th, 2012. Tate, we have found evidence of the missing girl's earring at your father's farmhouse property, are you involved in any way?'

'No, I am not, are you forgetting that Ally was my girlfriend and that I loved her. I haven't seen my father in about eight years.'

'Tate, we are going to fingerprint you. Have you known your father to kill in the past and you ever noticed anything suspicious when you were living there?'

'NO, NO, NO.'

'Okay, Tate. We are going to let you go home now, but we will be in touch so don't disappear.'

*   *   *

MIA SAT AT HER desk to review all her emails, since she had been working the ground the emails had built up. Making a cuppa and flicking open an email from the lab. The hair, blood, bone and skin that were taken in for evidence were confirmed as Ally's. Mia instantly felt sick, wondering what a horrible death Ally had gone through churned her stomach.

Mia shouted out across the room, 'John gather a crew. We are driving up to Joe's and arresting him. The DNA is a match to Ally. LET'S GO.'

*   *   *

TWO AND HALF HOURS later they arrived, knocking at Joe's door. There was no answer so they walked around the back to find Joe in one of the sheds.

'Joe, you are under arrest for the murder of Ally Gould. Anything you say can and will be held against you in a court of law.'

While Joe was being handcuffed, Joe's wife watched out the window, then the back door flung open and she was arrested. Both were put into the police cars and taken back to the station for questioning separately.

'Joe, the evidence came back positive from your mincer. Why did you murder Ally?'

'I want a smoke,' Joe said. They gave him a smoke, hoping he would talk. 'Was you wife your accomplice? Did she help murder Ally? Are there other victims? Where is Ally's body?'

'I want a coke,' Joe said. He got his coke. 'My wife had nothing to do with it. She knew I did it, but was not involved.' It was clear he had just realised that he just incriminated his wife as an accomplice, so he retracted his statement, 'No, she knew nothing of it.'

'Joe why? What was your motive for doing this?'

'Those girls who flaunt their bodies to men ask for trouble. They're no good people. I know his because my mother was in the adult industry and molested me – her boyfriends did as well. I was beaten then given Valium as a child, so I was mute most of the time. These kind of girls are all about themselves and don't give a shit about the world, other than making money for their filthy habits in life.'

'Joe how did you know what these girls did for work?'

'Tate told me.'

'Tate said he had not spoken to you in eight years?'

'Oh, he did, did he? We haven't seen each other in that long, but I call for his birthday, Easter, and Christmas.' Joe and his wife were locked up until sentencing.

KILLER STILL
AT LARGE

MIA RANG AVA TO gather everyone again, including Ally's mum. It was mid-morning and Mia decided to buy everyone coffee since she was delivering the unwelcome news to all.

Ava went out the front to help with all the coffee trays. All of them were in the lounge so Mia asked Pam if they could talk in the kitchen.

'Pam I am sorry to be the one to tell you this and my heart breaks for you, but the DNA was a match. It was Ally. Joe murdered her.

Pam released the loudest cry anyone had ever heard in their lives, Ava ran into the kitchen to see what happened. When she walked in the kitchen, she saw Pam collapsed on the floor and Ava guessed the news. Ava began crying herself and trying to comfort Pam. Twenty minutes had past and by then they were all in the kitchen.

Blade asked, 'Is Ally dead, Mia?'

'Yes, she is. I am so sorry for your loss. We have Joe and his wife arrested and locked up.' Everyone looked at Tate who was white as a ghost. Tate ran to the toilet to vomiting, he was in the toilet for at least fifteen minutes.

When he came out, Ivy gave him water to drink. 'Tate, can we talk in private please?' Mia asked.

Ava offered, 'You can go into our spare bedroom to talk if you'd like.'

'Tate, your dad Joe told us he killed Ally because of her work. His mother used to abuse him. Your nana was in the adult industry and he hated all women who were in the industry. He knew about her work and who she was because of a photo you sent him some time ago. At first, he thought it was just lost girls, which they were, but during the night he went through some photos for something to do and came across a picture of Ally and clicked who she was.'

'Mia, is he the serial killer?'

'We have no links or evidence to confirm he his.'

'Mia, I haven't seen him in eight years, but yes he has rang for special occasions and I did send a photo of Ally because I was so happy. She was my first love, I wanted to show them I had a girlfriend. I'm sorry for not saying this sooner.'

They were all sitting in silence and dumbfounded by what Tate and Mia had just recounted to them. They were crying and hugging each other, and all comforting Tate. Mia left the house, went back to the station and filled out her reports.

Ivy, Blade and Tate all said goodbye to each other and went home to process the news they just received.

*   *   *

MORNING CAME, IT WAS an odd day with storms, heavy rain, lightning and thunder. It was a cold but cosy day to stay safe and huddled in doors.

Ivy called Ava to see what time she was going to start her shift at work, and Ava replied, '10pm, Ivy, what about you?'

'Same, 10pm. See you there.'

Ivy and Ava went to bed to get sleep before their shifts.

*　*　*

PAM HESITANTLY WOKE UP late from a nap and called Ava. 'Ava now I know my Ally is dead. Oh my God, would you and

Ivy…' her speech was interrupted by her crying.

'Pam take deep breaths to calm yourself, take your time.' With a shiver in her voice Pam continued, 'Okay, Ava thank you. I would like your help with planning the funeral. Would that be ok?'

'Of course, Pam. Ivy and I will come to see you tomorrow around 3pm.'

'Okay, see you then.' Pam was feeling relieved that she has made the call and took a sleeping tablet to go to sleep. 'Ivy that was Pam.

She wants us to help her with the funeral, as you heard. I said we would be there tomorrow at 3pm, you good with that?'

'Okay of course.'

The night went on and the girls had a short night as there was less customers this evening. Ivy and Ava took their last break for the night, a total of fifteen minutes. They decided to sit at the bar to have a drink and chat about the funeral.

Ava suggested, 'White and purple flowers, as they were her favourite colours. And her favourite song, I Will Always Love You by Whitney Houston. I think Pam will let us plan it all, Ivy, as she is not in the right frame of mind. I mean who would be after losing a child. It doesn't feel right being here without Ally, she is a part of us, how do we move on without her?'

Ivy agreed, 'Ava have you noticed that man in the corner staring at us for ages now?'

'No!'

'Okay, let's keep talking and not make it noticeable that we aware of his stares, maybe I'm just paranoid.'

Ivy started to get up off her chair to start work again and as her feet hit the floor she looked around the room to see where she was going to get her next client, and she made eye contact with the man in the corner. He was moving his finger as if to say come over here.

'Ava, he wants me to come over. Keep an eye on me while I go over there.'

'Sure, go.'

Ivy took a seat in the booth where the man was, 'Hello, I'm Ivy. Were you calling for me to come over?'

'Hello Ivy. Yes, I was. I'm Jet. I have been watching you and your friend over there, you seem remarkably close to each other, and you are both great dancers.'

'Thank you, Jet. Yes, I did notice you staring, did you call me over for a reason or would you like a dance?

Can I have a private dance then I have a proposition?'

'Okay, Jet, please follow me to the private dance rooms.' Off they walked into a purple silk and velvet purple room. As soon as Ivy opened the door, she felt nothing but sadness as it was Ally's favourite room and colour. Ivy had to push those thoughts to the back of her head and focus on work.

'Come in, Jet, please take a seat. We take payment before we start.

'Yes, I know, I have been here before.'

'$100, thanks Jet.'

'Ivy, I'm going to pay you $500 for the three minute dance.' Ivy did not know what to think, was this a joke? And why does he look so familiar? She could not place his face from anywhere in the past, so she got back to focusing again.

'Jet, why are you paying me $500? What are you trying to prove?'

'We will talk after the dance.'

Jet paid his fee and Ivy put the music on. Her favourite song,

Ride My Pony came on. Ivy dressed up in a beautiful silver-sequence dress with her lingerie underneath and her 4-inch stilettos. Dancing seductively in front of Jet he seemed quite please.

Her dress came off, slowly dropping to the floor whilst Ivy's back was facing him. This left Ivy only in her lingerie and she bent over to touch her toes, moving her bum seductively. She could hear Jet moaning.

Flicking off her bra next and finishing her dance for Jet, looking directly into his eyes, Ivy paused took a deep breath in and felt her stomach get tingly. She got up, got dressed and stopped the music. She knew he was a good-looking guy, but why did she feel something while looking into his eyes. Get a grip girl. 'Ivy where can we talk in private and have your friend join us?'

'Follow me,

Jet.' As they walked out of the purple room a quick thought of Ally flashed through her mind again and right at that point Ivy got a chill that made her hairs stand up. Hmm that was weird. Walking through the club past the dance podiums towards the front of house there are booths, Ivy said, 'Jet take a seat in any booth and I will get my friend.'Jet went off to sit down and Ivy approached Ava.

'Ava I can't begin to tell you everything. His name is Jet, he is hot as, and he just paid me $500 for my three minute dance. Now he wants to talk to both of us, and he knows from watching us how close we are. He looks familiar but I don't know where from, Ava.'

'Yes, his face is familiar, but from where?'

'Okay, let's go so we don't hold him up.' Walking over to the booth Ivy said, 'I wonder what he could want to talk to us both about, hey.'

'Jet, this is Ava. Ava, Jet.'

'Hi, nice to meet you. Both of you take a seat next to each other in the booth,' Jet waved down the topless waiter over for a round of drinks. The drinks came quickly.

'So, what time do you both finish?' The girls looked at the time and said, 'Shit we are finished now, we need to clock off. Sorry Jet, we will be back in a minute.'

'Sure, take your time girls.'

Ivy and Ava quickly changed into their normal clothes and clocked off. It was 1am and they were tired but were intrigued to find out what Jet had to say.

'Sorry Jet, we are off the clock now. So, what is the proposition?'

'Okay Ivy, so you know I'm good for money, yes?'

'Yes, okay you proved that.'

'Well I work for someone, let's just say he's classed as a billionaire. His birthday is coming up and I am on the lookout for talented dancers for entertainment.'

'Oh, sorry,' said Ava. 'We don't hire ourselves out.' Ivy said, 'Ava, let's hear him out.'

'Yes. Okay, okay. Go ahead Jet, sorry.'

'Alright I cannot reveal who I work for as they are in government, I know you do not know me, but you must trust me I have to work with confidentiality for my client. If you accept the offer, then you will see who I work for and you will have to sign a confidentiality form to not speak of this again to anyone when the night has finished.'

Ivy was starting to get a little excited, Ava not so much. They could not believe what they were hearing.

Ava was sceptical, so asked, 'What do we get out of this Jet? What would we get payed, and that is not saying I am interested.'

'What you both get out of this is $20,000 each.' Both of their mouths dropped open, Ava stopped breathing for a second and Ivy's eyes lit up like a Christmas tree.

Ava, trying to be serious and straight faced, said, 'Do you have a business card with your number on it, as we need to go home and gather our thoughts. It's been a long night considering it was meant to be an early one.'

'Of course, I do.'

'When is event meant to be, Jet?'

'Next weekend on Saturday night, I would want you both to be there early to mingle with the guests. You will both need to be dressed extremely formal, as the night continues we will give you the indication to go and change into your costumes for dancing for the guests. One thing I left out is that you will be giving lap dances to whomever requires one… But you will both do a double act for the birthday boy. You will have 24 hours to think this through before the offer is off the table.

Clearly we can find other dancers; they are not in short supply in this town.'

'Well we have a friend's funeral on Saturday morning, but you are not in need of us until night time,' Ava confirmed. 'Oh, sorry to hear that, can I ask how someone so young passed?'

'She has been killed by a lunatic,' said Ava with tears in her eyes.

'Oh, that is horrible. I am sorry again, it was not from the serial killer that is killing all the young girls was it?'

'No, the girl was murdered out of town by a madman, they do not think he is the serial killer. Okay Jet, nice to meet you. We will let you know tomorrow, I guess, thanks for asking,' Ivy said, laughing slightly. As she walked off she looked back to wave and Jet winked at her and she got giddy.

Ava went home to Jax and Ivy to Blade. By this time, it was 3am.

Ava disturbed Jax when she got into bed, 'Why are you so late in, I thought it was an early night.'

'Go to sleep, Jax. I will tell you in the morning.'

Morning came, Blade was up and had flicked on the T.V, put the kettle on and was waiting in the kitchen. He decided he wanted toast as well. It was about 10am and Ivy could smell the toast, slowly opening her eyes, yawning and lying in bed for a minute trying to comprehend the night and the offer that was made and knowing she had to tell Blade but didn't know how to.

Scuffling out of bed, finally, she stumbled through to the kitchen. 'Hi bab e.'

'Morning hun, coffee, toast?'

'Yes please.' Plonking herself at the table waiting for her breakfast, she heard the T.V. on in the background, listening to the morning show that was on the channel.

'Toast and coffee are ready, let's have breakfast in the lounge watching T.V. this morning.

'Okay,' said Ivy. Sitting on the couch, sipping coffee contemplating her day ahead with Pam and the night before, with Jet,

Ivy stared into space.

'So why did you come home so late, Ivy? Was Ava late home to?'

'Yes, we did finish work early but there is something I must tell you Blade…'

'I am intrigued, do tell.'

'Well I did a dance for a client, and he paid me $500 and then said I would like to talk to you and your friend after the dance.'

'WHAT!'

'Yes, that's what I thought too. Ava was hesitant, but we listened to what he had to say we all talked for 2 hours. Anyway, he works for someone in Government and this person has a birthday coming up and he is on the lookout for entertainment. He approached us and asked us if we would be interested There are a few rules: come early to mingle, then perform and sign a confidential agreement to not to speak of the night in question or who it was for.'

'And what did you say?'

'I didn't say anything, but Ava told him we do not hire ourselves out for parties, but babe you want to know what the highlight is? We will get $20,000 each! And he wants an answer in 24 hours, well from last night so he will call us tonight for our decision.'

Bade spat out his coffee, '$20,000 for how long?'

'A couple of hours, babe. What should I do?'

'Okay Ivy, I have heard everything you have had to say, now it's my turn. Realistically you do not know this man, you do not know if he's telling you the truth, and because you are not allowed to give out information, I'm not comfortable not knowing where you will be. If something happens, how will I help you. There is a serial killer on the loose and you do not know how many men you are entertaining for without security.'

'Hold on, babe, he gave us a card let me show you. Written on it is: Jet Simons GOVERNMENT SECURITY PERSONAL ASSISTANT 396584527.'

'Ivy anyone can make up business cards and go into your place of work just to try and pick up girls.'

'Yeah, I know babe, but I feel his legit.'

'So, what? You want to do this gig? When is it?'

'Next Saturday.'

That's Ally's funeral.'

'Yes, I know but that is in the morning.'

'I don't feel good about this Ivy, and if Ava is not going to do it then neither are you okay. The money is great and could be house deposit for us, but your life is more valuable to me, Ivy.'

'Okay, I am going to Pam's at 3 pm and meeting Ava there to talk about the funeral arrangements, and I will talk to her then.

* * *

PAM HEARD KNOCKING AT her front door, it was Ivy and Ava.

'Come in girls. I will put the kettle on, thank you for helping me I do not know where to start.'

'Pam we will have purple and white flowers, we will have her favourite love song – I Will Always Love You – by Whitney Houston, we will contact Tobin Brothers and they do all the organising for us, is that okay?' Ava asked?

'Yes, girls, thank you. I miss her so much girls. Just her quirkiness, you know.'

'Yes, we felt her absence at work, it's so cruel that she was taken when she had her whole life ahead of her. Pam are you okay with having guests here to eat afterwards?' Ivy asked.

'That's okay as I will need to be around people, I think.'

'Ava did you tell Jax about last night?' Ivy asked.

'Yes, and he is not happy for me to do it because I can't disclose the address. But the money has got him thinking and he said I can't go if you don't. He won't let me go alone but the final decision is mine. What do we do, Ivy, he is going to call us tonight when we are at work wanting our answer? It is such a scary time we are living in right now with a serial killer out there and we don't know Jet at all, but if he is in the security business for Government you would think we would be safe right?'

'Okay, we will do it and the moment we finish we get out and call Jax to pick us up.'

'Okay, decision made.'

'Pam were going to leave now and plan Ally's funeral. We will see you on Saturday morning,' said Ava.

'Thanks again, girls.'

Arranging the funeral was emotional for the girls, as they had to put a video and photo collection together for the display, and music which pulls at your heart strings. Ava decided to draft a short poem dedicated to Ally to read while other people making speeches.

Ally you where the light in our day Now we sit here and pray.

You made people laugh

And follow your path Your kind-hearted soul You made our lives whole.

*   *   *

IVY AND AVA ARRIVED at work that night, it was a Thursday and the crowd was rocking with a lot of clients – they were in for a busy night.

It was Ava's turn to be dancing on the podium and it was around 12.30 am and she spotted a familiar face in the crowd, it was Jet. She tried to get Ivy's attention, but could not. Jet sat in the booths until the girls went on break.

Ava finished her dance time slot and said to Ivy, 'Come on it is break time.' Ivy got down. 'Ivy, Jet is here. I thought he was going to ring us?'

'Shit I am nervous, Ava.'

'Me too, but we can change our mind, you know.'

'Hi Jet. We thought you were going to ring us,' Ivy asked. 'Well I wanted to see you face-to-face, girls. And if you say no well, I am in the right place to approach other dancers.'

Okay, Jet we have decided to take your offer. But as soon as we have finished entertaining, we are leaving.'

'Okay,' Jet said. He immediately got on his phone. 'Ivy, Ava, what are your bank details?'

They handed over their details to Jet hesitantly, holding their breath and wondering what they were doing.

'One-minute girls, please,' Jet said as he was on his phone. 'There done.'

'What?'

'The $20,000 is in your banks now, check if you like, I will sit here while you go to your dressing rooms to check your bank.'

Off they went to retrieve their phones, opening their bank details they couldn't believe this was true and happening. There they both had $20,000 each in their account.

'OH my God, Ava, can you believe this?' Ivy asked. 'No, I am speechless. Let's go back to Jet.'

'Jet it's in our banks, thank you for paying us prior to event,' Ava said, confirming.

'Well I am sure you thought it was fraud or something.'

'Yes, we were and still are uneasy about it all,' Ava agreed.

'Okay girls I must leave now see you Saturday, I have your address and a limo will pick you up Ava first at 5 pm Saturday and then on to get you, Ivy.' Before they could say anything, Jet was out of the booth and out of the building.

The girls went back to work for another hour. When worked finished and they were walking back to the car Ava asked, 'Ivy did you give him our addresses? How does he know our addresses?'

'I don't know, Ava. I don't think I did but I cannot honestly remember.' Mm thought Ava.

WALKING INTO UNCHARTED TERRITORY

SATURDAY MORNING COMES AND all the people gathered at the church for Ally's funeral. Quite a turn out of people to pay their respects, and a lot of girls from Ally's work industry came along with their parents who came to support Pam.

The ceremony went beautifully, Ava read her poem and people were grabbing tissues from their pockets and handbags. Tears flowed throughout the church. The flowers looked gorgeous and the happy photos of Ally made into a video made the guests cry and laugh. After the ceremony, all followed the hearse to the cemetery for the burial. The sun was shining with only a few clouds, a slight breeze and the birds chirping putting life into the cemetery.

Arriving at the burial site, Blade caught site of Tate and waved for him to gather with them. Tate made his way over to the group and hugged Pam; he wasn't planning on coming because he hadn't known how he would be treated and did not know if his friends and Pam would accept him being there.

Pam said, 'I am glad you are here Tate. This is not your fault, Tate how where you to know? You cannot carry this burden on your shoulders.'

'Thank you, Pam that means so much. I loved her so much.'

The burial began and more tears flowed, as the coffin dropped into the 6ft hole. Some guests threw dirt and others threw flowers. A white butterfly landed on Ava's shoulder and she just broke down crying, she took it as a sign that it was Ally. Ally always believed that white butterflies were angels, so this was a sign that she was okay in Ava's eyes. In that moment she felt strangely at peace. And for that same reason Pam felt at peace for the first time since Ally's death. All the guest's headed back to Pam's for food and to celebrate Ally's short life.

Ally would want everyone to be celebrating her life, not being sad because it was over, that was the type of girl she was.

Tate got a plate of food and sat with the group chatting away. They all spoke about the positives that Ally brought into their lives. Then Jax asked Tate, 'Have you heard from Mia? Do you know if your dad is the serial killer? Have you gone to visit him for an exclamation?'

'I did go to see him; it was the hardest thing I have had to do in my life. Got there and his face was pale with a cold, hard stare. I did not even recognise my own father, he had no remorse. When I asked him why, he replied "tramps don't deserve to live, the serial killer is doing a good job". I just got up and walked out, I was disgusted that my parents had this hate in them and the one person I loved most in the world they took away. I can't understand my parents are murderers, I cannot grasp it.'

They all stood up to hug Tate, had a drink and cheered to Ally. Just as they put their cups down, Mia walked into Pam's house to pay her respects and to speak with Tate.

Mia approached Pam and said, 'I am sorry I missed the funeral, but I am sure it was beautiful.'

'Yes, Mia thank you. It was thanks to the girls.'

'Tate may I have a word with you in private?'

'Yes, sure Mia.' They walked to the front of the house.

'Tate, I just wanted to inform you that your dad, Joe is not the serial killer. This was a one-off from what we have concluded, not that it makes it any easier for you knowing that your dad killed your girlfriend because of her profession.'

'Thanks, Mia, for the update. I am glad they're in prison for life. I know that they will die in there, but some girls may be that bit safer with them off the streets.' Mia left and Tate went back into the house to say good-bye to everyone, he felt drained.

Blade yelled out to for him to come by anytime as he drove off. Everyone else said their farewells and headed home as Ivy and Ava had a big night ahead and wanted to get sleep before the gig.

*   *   *

AVA WOKE UP AT 3 pm and rang Ivy to make sure she was awake as well. She was, 'See you at 5, Ivy.' At 5pm the doorbell rang and Jax got up to open the door to find a tall, dark, handsome man formally dressed in a tuxedo. As Jax looked passed the man's shoulder he saw a limo in the street, Ava came from out of the bedroom as Jax looked her way he felt uneasy.

'You look beautiful, Ava. Be aware and alert, and call me when you finish and I will pick you up straight away. Do you have your pepper spray?'

'Yes, Jax. I love you and will call you later.'

Taking a seat in the limo, Ava felt quite impressed. Music was playing and there was sparkling champagne with two glasses, obviously for Ivy and herself. Popping open the bottle of champagne and pouring a glass for herself, bouncing her head to the music on the radio, she felt relaxed and happy. I feel great what could go wrong tonight? Was this still the right decision… Yes, everything will be fine.

'Driver the address for Ivy is…' Ava was interrupted.

'Yes, ma'am I know where to go, thank you.' Again, that thought of not knowing if Ivy gave Jet their address or not bothered Ava. Ten minutes later the driver got out and went to Ivy's front door. Blade answered and was not amused at how good looking this driver was. Looking past the driver, Blade saw Ava waving to him from out the window, waving back he yelled, 'Be careful.'

Ivy already ready, walked out the door, kissed Blade and said, 'Love you, I will see you later.'

'Here Ivy, have a drink to relax,' Ava offered.

'I need it, thanks.' They were discussing the events of day, the funeral and general chit chat while driving to a place they had no idea about.

'Where do think we are going, do you think it will be a mansion, Ava?'

'I don't know, Ivy. I am nervous and excited at the same time.'

'Yes so am I.' Sitting in silence they tried to gather their thoughts, the 5.30 pm news came on the radio.

There has been another woman found just out of town. Murdered, raped, and tortured, her body had been found off an old country road heading out of town. Holding their breath, they looked at each other with uneasiness, gulped their champagne and refilled their glasses.

'My gosh, Ava. No women have been found in a while, I thought the killer was caught or something.'

Driving out of the suburbs down highways towards more country towns, Ava spoke to the driver, 'Where are you taking us?'

'Cannot tell you that ma'am, you know that.' The driver continued driving, and took a turn off exit off the highway. Now they were really in the country, forest on each side of the road with little dirt tracks running of the main road. Up ahead they all saw bright lights flashing.

'What is that?' Ivy asked the driver.

'I am not sure we are going past it shortly, we will know when we get closer.'

They drove closer to all the lights and slowed down as directed there where night lights as it started getting dark, crime scene tape, police everywhere. 'Oh no! Bet it is the girl they just found. When is this ever going to stop, the police are not working hard enough, how many more girls must die before they catch him? How can this killer leave no evidence at all, I do not get it, Ava?' Five minutes down the road they came to a stop, they parked in the front of the biggest cast iron gates they had ever seen in their life. Beside them was a box that the driver spoke into.

The driver pressed the buzzer and waited for an answer. It was crackly then, 'Hello, hello?'

'Hello, it is Paul Driver with the entertainment.' Ivy laughed, as his name was fitting for his job. Looking out the window in amazement they watched the big gates slowly open for them to drive through.

'Wow!' screeched Ivy. 'Have you ever seen anything like this, Ava? Tennis courts, golf course, pool, spas, gyms… what is this place?'

'Who owns it you mean, Ivy. I am getting nervous…'

Pulling up to the front door they saw a man waiting there ready to guide them into the mansion. The girls jumped out, grabbing all their bags with costumes in them.

'Good evening, ladies. Welcome to the home of Trish Jones, please follow me and I will lead you to your rooms.'

Now feeling a bit more excited, the girls walked through the large double front doors, entered a foyer with the grandest stairs they had ever seen with gold handrails, chandeliers and polished floors. The view took their breath away.

Walking up the stairs to the room they were given to get ready for the night. They were given instructions to freshen up and someone would come to get them in thirty minutes to mingle with the crowd. The door closed behind them, it was the first time they felt they could breathe properly.

'God, look at this room, Ivy. It's bigger than my home with a canopy king size bed, 16 ft ceilings, one wall all mirrored, a bathroom with twin sinks, shower, spa, lushest green ferns and a view out the window of the forest to die for.' Ava put on the T.V, but on mute and put on the radio loud to get into the vibe for the night ahead. Discussing and practicing their dance routine as they promised to dance a double act together. Ava and Ivy sent a quick message to Jax and Blade saying I love you and we will see you soon. Ping. They both got the same response back – be careful. They were starting to feel numb with a little more wine in them than they should have had to calm the nerves, plus they had to drink more when they were to go downstairs to mingle.

Their outfits were on, makeup and hair done, another glass of wine, a quick smoke shared between them – they don't smoke all time just on the odd occasion.

Knock.

'This is it, Ivy. I think I will be glad when this is all over even though I needed this money.' Ava walked over to the large double doors with gold doorknobs.

'Hello ladies, are you ready to come down and blend in with the crowd?'

'Yes, let's start the night.' Walking down a lavish hallway towards the top of the stairs, they stopped to look at each other and take a deep breath. 'Are you okay, ladies?'

'Yes, we are okay, thank you. Just catching out breath.' Slowly walking down the stairs careful not to trip in their long sparkly gown's with high heels, they finally reached the bottom.

'Follow me ladies.' Turning to the right down another large hallway, wondering where they were going, they came to a halt in front of another set of double doors which where double the size of the room upstairs.

As he pulled one side of the door open, there was so many people, around 300 Ava guessed. A band was playing on a large stage, the sound in the room was so loud with all these guests talking, it was like being at a concert. Lavish dressed tables with fine china and gourmet food served at tables, served on gold platers by waiters and servers.

Before they knew it, they were left alone in the crowd, not knowing who to talk to so they stood to one side of the room with wine in one hand and a quiche in the other, admiring the size of the room.

'Who knows this amount people, Ava?' The band stopped playing for a brief time and a spokesperson got on stage.

'Ladies and gentlemen. I would like to thank you for being here tonight to celebrate the 60th birthday of the commissioner, Jack Jones. Put your hands together.'

With everyone clapping the noise was extremely loud, the room echoed. 'Ava, we are at a police commissioner's birthday.'

'Yes, Ivy and I thought I briefly saw the state premier here. They are all top knobs in the highest of industries here to celebrate.'

'Bloody hell, Ava. We are dancing for the extremely rich, no wonder they could pay us that much.'

'Let's go to the bar for another drink, I am going to drink something stiffer.'

'Yes, me too,' agreed Ivy. While ordering their drinks, the heard the commissioner say, 'There is more entertainment coming up in twenty mins, do not go anywhere. You will not want to miss this. Thank you all for coming and I hope you have an enjoyable night.'

The band started to play eighties and nineties music.

Ivy gulping, started to cough as the drink went down the wrong hole. Ava was laughing. 'Far out, we are on in twenty minutes,' Ivy complained.

Ava said, 'Look at the bright side, we get to go home real soon.'

'Ladies would you mind going to get ready for your performance, I will be up in twenty minutes to collect you.' As they started to walk off towards the doors, they spotted Mia in the crowd waving at them, with a shocked look on her face. They could see Mia trying to make her way over to them, but they just waved back and kept walking.

'Shit we must dance in front of these high-profile people, half of which are police and in parliament. Now we must dance half-naked in front of someone we know well.'

'Just keep walking, Ava, or we will not have time to freshen up.' Ivy walked ten more steps, and felt something under her shoe. She looked down and saw she had stood on some food that had been dropped.

'Aww,' Ivy commented. She took another step and bumped into someone, and as she was apologising she looked up and stood there frozen.

'Rise? Oh my God, Rise, what are you doing here?'

'I could ask the same for you girls.'

'Fuck,' Ava said. 'Rise we cannot talk we have to go.' Ivy took one look back before they closed the door and noticed a dance pole was being fixed to the roof for them to dance on. Off they went to the room to change and freshen up.

'Fuck… Fuck… Fuck… I don't know if I can pull myself together to dance in front of Mia and Rise, can you Ava? The other 298 people we do not know so I do not give a shit, but the two we know makes it worse.'

'Okay Ivy, calm down. We have been paid to do this, you got this girl. Just wipe them out of your mind and start to focus on me and our dance.' Walking off to change and freshen up Ivy came out of the room, 'Okay, Ava. Yes, I got this. Let's do it and go home.'

Coming down the stairs, they turning right into the long, wide hallway. The big doors opened and all stopped and looked their way, as they were not wearing any clothes. Making their way up to the stage, making eye contact with Mia and passing Rise, wondering if they knew each other at all.

Arriving at the stage there was an announcement for the call up of the commissioner to come to the stage to take a seat. He did so promptly, with a big fat smile on his face and droplets of sweat dripping from his forehead which made the girls want to puke.

The lights dimmed, the music started and they began their erotic dance together. Kissing, touching, bending, and crawling over the stage with one another. They took off the top layer of clothes and were left in lingerie. Ava was in see-through lace panties and a bra. Ivy was in white which glowed in the dim lights.

They soon parted, and Ava climbed the dance pole to swing and perform on, while Ivy went over to the commission, leant on his knees and bent over to show him her cleavage. Then she got up, turned her back to him, bending over so he could see her fine arse from behind. When Ivy stood up her bra was undone and she flicked it into the crowd and it landed on Rise, who was happy about that. Dancing on the commissioner with her boobs in his face, smiling like he had won tattslotto.

He tried to grab her boobs but she said, 'No, you can't touch me, that's the deal.' Then Ava came down off the pole, danced toward Ivy and then they kissed again. Ivy swirled Ava around and unclipped her bra, and flung it onto the commissioner. He tucked it in his pocket, while they continued to dance and tease the commissioner, with Ivy pretending to take off Ava's panties. The crowd was going crazy, screaming 'TAKE THEM OFF, TAKE THEM OFF.'

While they were dancing Ivy was playing with Ava's boobs, 'What do we, Ava?'

'We will do it quickly, you take mine off, I will take yours off, then we will kiss, and you go behind, while I go in front of the birthday boy and end our dance.'

They did just that, their dance ended, and they walked off the stage. The crowd was yelling, 'MORE, MORE, MORE.' They were not going to do any more.

'What a relief, I am so glad we are finished.'

*　*　*

ONCE OFF THE STAGE they went ahead to walk up to the room to change and call Jax to pick them up. As Ava was about to call

Jax there was a knock at the door. Ivy went to open it and it was the commissioner.

'Hello ladies, I just wanted to thank you for your entertainment. I believe all my guests enjoyed your performance' I would like to put a proposal to you both for further engagements in the future and the payout for your entertainment would be around the $50,000 mark.'

Ava put her hand under Ivy's jaw as it fell open with astonishment, 'Thank you, commissioner, you have given us something to think about. I know you have our details and I am sure you will send someone to contact us when in need we will give you an answer. We hope you enjoyed your birthday.'

Ivy was about to shut the door, felt it swing back open and was Rise standing in the doorway.

'Ladies! Wow! What a performance, no wonder the commissioner was sweating. You danced like queens for him, and us. Have not seen you girls perform so intimately like that b efore.'

'Well for that kind of money we had to pull out the stops. Rise, we heard about another death on our way in here tonight have you heard any more about it? We passed it, it is close to this mansion,' Ivy demanded.

'Yes, it shook people up being close to the commissioner's home. We will know more by Monday when the autopsy reports come through.'

'Rise, it has been a year and you all have not got any closer to finding the killer, how hard could it be, Rise?' Ava asked angrily.

'As I said girls this person is so professional, we do not believe he is working alone. You cannot tell anyone.'

'Look where we are, Rise, we are at a confidential party. We know how to keep quiet,' Ivy retorted.

'It is like Ted Bundy running around the streets again.'

'Okay, Rise. We want to leave now, we have had a long night,' Ava stated. 'Okay, girls see you again.'

Ava messaged Jax: meet us down the highway at 2 am, the driver will take us to the servo just before the exit. Meet you their baby.

Okay, Jax Replied.

The driver came to the bedroom door, 'Girls are you ready to leave?'

'Yes sir, we are,' confirmed Ivy. Off they went down to the limo. The night air was cold they huddled together until the warmth of the heater touched their tired faces.

No help in sight

It was dark and eerie coming out of the driveway of the mansion that was based in the deep of the forest, as most of the guests flashy cars had left by now and there were no lights on the driveway. There were no lights or roads other than tracks surrounding the huge amount of acreage this place was on. Once they passed the large gates a sense of relief fell upon them.

Dozing off in the back of the limo, they heard a noise and they jumped in surprise. it was the glass divider between the driver and the girls, it had opened up. It was soundproof but they did not know it. They thought nothing of it, until Ivy looked out the window and realised that they should have been on the highway by now – in civilisation – but they were not. It seemed that they were deeper in the forest, they now had no idea where the hell they were.

'Ava, fuck where are we?'

'I don't know, Ivy.' Ava moved to the front of the limo and started banging on it but the driver didn't move. He just kept driving, the driver ignored them.

'Oh my God, Ava! Try to ring Jax quick we have been kidnapped.'

Ava quickly pulled out her phone, dialling Jax, 'Hello, JAX IT'S AVA WE ARE KIDNAPPED, HELP FIND US WE DON'T KNOW WHERE … BEEP, BEEP, BEEP…'

Ava's service ran out, they were so far into the forest, they could not get a signal on their phone.

'Shit, shit, shit! Hey driver, where are we going?' they got no response. Ivy started crying, Ava went back to the backseat to hug her.

'Oh my God, Ava we are going to die! Where are they taking us? Why us?

Why won't he listen, could these be the people killing all the girls? I'm not ready to die, I have plans for a wonderful fulfilled life with Blade and to have kids.'

'Ivy have you got your pepper spray in your bag?'

'Yes.'

'Me too, we may have to use it. I know we are tired and have had a long night, but it just may get longer and now we need to be alert more than ever. OUR LIVES DEPEND ON IT OKAY. Whatever happens Ivy, as we may be separated.'

'Oh no!'

'Yes, and may be do not fight them, it will make things worse for you, promise me.'

'Yes okay.'

'Whatever happens, if we get locked in a room always remember that I will not give up on trying to escape and to come and save you, always keep the hope.'

'Love you, and I feel blessed you are in my life, Ava. You are so strong minded; I wish I were like you, Ava.'

'Shush now.'

The limo came to an abrupt halt, before they had time to blink or think what to do, the door flung open and a man all in black and a black balaclava ripped Ava out of the limo placing a bag over her head immediately. Ivy automatically screamed in fear for her life. A second man came in and ripped Ivy out of the limo and placed a bag on her head also. Ivy automatically put up a small fight, it was her natural reaction, until thoughts of Ava popped into her head. Do not fight them Ivy, that calmed her a little. They were made to walk fast, tripping over the branches and twigs and rocks that covered a forest floor. The chill in the air was probably down to 6 degrees by now, they were freezing. Their bags where left in the limo as they did not have the time to grab them as they were pulled out of the car so quickly. Walking for what seemed like fifteen minutes felt like three hours to the girls. They heard a squeaky door open and when they went through it, it felt like cobwebs had brushed past their hands. It gave them the chills. 'We are coming up to steps,' said a voice. 'We are going to go down them and I will hold you until we get to the bottom.' Walking down two flights of stairs, it felt colder again the further they went down.

They got to the bottom and then they were thrown to the ground, landing on an old, torn smelly mattress. They could hear water drops dripping in the closeness of the room, not far from them.

A voice said, 'No screaming, there is a torch on the mattress you will have to find it. Do not take off the bags on your head until you hear the door shut, that is when we have left the room. When you hear the door open again and every other time, you will place the bags on your head. Do you understand?'

Whimpering, they both agreed.

The door closed and at the same time, they took off the bags from their heads.

'Ava, I'm sorry I screamed. It just came out.'

'That's okay, we are together that's good. Feel around for a torch, Ivy.' They were both feeling around and found torches. Turning on the torch was a great relief to have light, even though the torches kept flickering.

'Sweet Jesus, we are in a basement with leaky pipes, there is dirty rat's and spiders. Not to mention this disgusting mattress. What do they want with us, we have nothing they want?' Ivy asked.

'I don't know.' Slowly moving the torch around the room, Ava came across a locked, old wooden door that was bolted.

She walked over to it and tried fiddling with the lock, then out of nowhere she heard hello, 'Is somebody there?'

Sucking in her breath while looking at Ivy, whispering 'Did you hear that?'

'Yes, it sounded like a girl.'

Ava knocked on the door, 'Hello, is someone in there?'

'Yes, my name is Hannah. Who are you?'

'We are Ava and Ivy. There is two of us. Hannah how long have you been here?'

'I don't know, three months or so.'

'Fuck,' said Ivy. 'Months?'

'Yes, I have been tortured, raped and abused. My has body used for their pleasure, and they barely give me any food to eat. I don't know how much more I can take. I would rather be dead at this point.' God, is this our fate, the girls wondered, is this how our lives end?

'Hannah when they come to you do you see their faces? Do they come through this door to you?'

'No, Ava, there is another door in here they come through. And I see no faces they wear beanie-looking things.'

'Okay,' Ava said to the girls. 'We are all in this together. Hannah do you know if there are any other girls?'

'When I was first brought here, I heard other girl's voices and cries, but they have fallen silent over the last few weeks. I think they have died or been killed.'

'Hannah, do you have a phone? Any kind of communication with the outside?'

'NO! would I be here if I did?'

'Sorry that was a stupid question, ours is out in the limo. With our bags.'

'Well you won't see them again. Shush!' said Hannah. 'Someone is coming my way.' Hannah's door opened, and three men brutally walked in with ties in their hands. One tied her legs, the other tied her arms, and then the other raped her while the others watched. Ava and Ivy could hear her screams of pain, and begging them to stop.

One man then slapped her face and said, 'shut up you stupid bitch.' Then the other two took their turn and had their way with her.

'I need water and food,' Hannah cried. The men just left and slammed the door.

Thirty minutes passed, and someone was knocking on Hannah's door. They all tensed. The big, solid wooden door squeaked opened and a tray with water and a sandwich was flung across the room. Hannah crawled on her hands and knees, drank the water and ate the sandwich in seconds. She was so hungry, it was her first bit of food in four days.

'They have no mercy, Ava. They haven't even begun to torture us yet, I am so scared.'

'I am too. I need to go to the toilet, where do I go?' Looking around with the torch they found an empty bucket; they had no choice but to use it.

The door slammed opened in the room where Ivy and Ava were huddled together frightened. They must have fallen asleep because the door opening startled them.

'Here, some water and sandwich. Eat,' said one man. 'Please could we get a blanket?' Ivy asked.

'What do you think this is, a motel? Shut the fuck up.' They left as quick as they came. To their relief they got food and not a beating, eating the sandwich and savouring every mouthful as they didn't know when they would eat again.

'It must be morning, Ivy. I wonder how long we slept for.' Ivy knocked on the locked door that lead into Hannah's room to see if she was awake.

'Hannah are you awake?' No answer. She was still sleeping. About two hours went by but they had no way to make out the time. They felt dirty and wanted and needed a shower. Ivy tried to knock on the door again, 'Hannah are you there?' Nothing.

'Oh, Ava, what has happened to her?'

The door slammed open again and the men walked straight over to the locked door that lead to Hannah's.

A man opened it and said, 'You,' pointing to Ava. 'Get in here now.' Ava got up and looked at Ivy as if to say do not fight them. Ava shoved hard through the door so fast that she fell to the ground. She got up but was pushed back down. In this room there was a dim light and she could see better ,but she wished she couldn't because what she saw looking around the room and the stench in there nearly made her sick.

There was blood all over the walls, and what looked like fingernail scratches on the floor, and she could see chipped broken fingernails. They have killed Hannah.

'What do you want from us?' shrieked Ava.

'Shut up.' Ivy jumped as the door opened in her room and she didn't know what to expect. Another two men came in and walked straight through to the next door to where Ava was, Ivy gulped and held her breathe. The door slammed hard. Ava was so frighted, within seconds, Ava had her clothes torn off. One man at either end spread her legs and arms, pinning her to the bloodied floor. Ava tried not to scream, as she knew it would freak out Ivy, but she could not help it. A big, large man with a mask on jammed himself inside Ava and she let out the loudest scream. Ivy cried and froze.

The big man finished his business and another masked man said, 'Turn her over now.'

Ava turned over and started screaming, 'Please no! Please do not do this!' One of the men holding her leg said, 'Scream again and you will lose a finger. That will give you something to scream about.'

Ava was savagely raped from behind, they had split her and there was blood everywhere. She screamed twice as loud as before, then fell silent. Ivy thought she was dead. Ava passed out, as they cut her finger off because of her screaming.

The door swung open and they said, 'You,' to Ivy. 'Get in there now.' Ivy moved like she never had before in her life. Pushing Ivy through the door, she fell also, they door slammed shut.

'Ava, oh my god. What have they done to you?'

Not moving, Ivy started hugging her and looking around to see all the blood everywhere. She could not believe what she was seeing. Ivy then noticed that there was blood pouring out of Ava, but could not work out where until she picked up her hand to hold it. She saw that they cut off a finger, and she noticed her bum was covered in blood. Ivy got one of Ava's socks and wrapped her finger up to try to help stop the bleeding.

Ava slowly came to, 'Ivy what are you doing in here?'

'Oh Ava, they put me in here a little while ago. You have passed out.' Ava tried to sit up but her body was riddled with pain. She was coming to realise they raped her.

Putting her hand up to wipe her forehead, 'Ivy why is my sock on my finger?' Unravelling the sock, she looked at the space were her finger used to be and nearly fainted again. Ivy wrapped it back up. Who are these monsters, where is Hannah? All these questions with no answers.

'Ivy, these men are the serial killers as the girls that were found, were found with body parts missing, this is the same and they were all raped as well.

We must get out of here, I pray that Jax has gone for help. We must hope Jax has called Mia or Rise and gone to the police to report us missing.

Please Jax, come through for us. Ivy, we could be here for months, years, nobody knew the address we were at and we were not in our car. The leads are only going to take searched to the servo where I told Jax to meet us. Mia and Rise know that we were at the party so that may give them a bit of a lead to focus closer to the house, they can interview some of the police that were there but they could all deny seeing us too. If we are dealing with dirty and corrupt police officers, Ivy, we are dead girls.' They hugged each other and cried.

*   *   *

JAX WENT TO THE police station to tell them that the girls didn't turn up at the servo at the time they said they would be there. Jax also told them that he got the strangest call from Ava, saying they have been kidnapped, they didn't know where they were, and he had heard screaming then the phone cut out more than likely due to lack of service in the area.

'Jax I will make a report and hand it immediate over to the detectives, you will hear from us soon.'

Jax went home and decided to call Mia, he knew he should not but so what? Mia took the call from Jax and went straight over to his house.

Mia turned up in fifteen minutes, Jax opened the door and let her in. 'Hi Jax, what is going on?'

'I have just left the police station and reported Ava and Ivy missing, I waited for them at the servo up near Woodend exit and I received a strange call from Ava screaming, "I think we are kidnapped, don't know where we are" and the phone cut out, due to lack of service.'

'Oh my God, okay Jax this is bad this could be the serial killer. Tell me where were they coming from, Jax?'

'I don't know, Mia. That is why I was at the servo, I was not told their location. They went to a private party to entertain and were paid $20,000, each to perform, all I was told that it had something to do with a high honcho in government and it was a birthday party and they signed a contract of confidentiality.'

'Sweet Jesus, Jax. I was there I saw them, and Rise was there too. I didn't know they knew him, so they left the function and didn't make it to the servo. I saw them leave with the limo driver about 2am, the servo is what, twenty minutes from the location of disappearance. Okay, Jax this case will come through to me today if you have reported it, I will not say anything. I will work the case by the books, but I will also work it behind the scenes. I will keep you informed, you must not tell anyone. We may be dealing with dirty police officers here, and I need to be discreet. I will organise a search party from the servo onwards to the last location they were seen at. I'm going to head into the office now, Jax, can I come back tonight? I may or may not have updates.'

'Okay, sure see you later.' Jax and Mia looked at each other before Mia walked out the door, their eyes connected in a strange fleeting moment of unsureness. Mia snapped out of it and got into her car started the engine and drove off.

Talking to herself, what was that about Mia? Why did you look into this young handsome man's deep eyes? Why did you feel something when you did? I do not even like guys, I have a wonderful female partner, I love her very much. Mia was trying to convince herself otherwise.

*   *   *

MIA ARRIVED AT THE office, made a coffee and sat at her desk that is full of other murder files. She opened her emails and of course she was on the case as she knew she would be. The T.V. was on in the office and somehow the media got ahold of this information that Ava and Ivy were missing. How? How could they know this already?

A commercial came on the T.V. which gave Mia time to think. Collapsing her head into her hands, she wiped her eyes, then got back to focusing.

Okay, I need to find out the limo driver's name as he would be a suspect, being the last one to see them. Mia made calls to the right-hand man of the commissioner so to speak. She was a female, Mia grunted, not believing that Trish was right for the job. There was something off about her.

'Hello Trish, it is Mia here. Can you tell me the name of the limo driver that picked up and took the girls after the party the other night.' Trish was silent on the other end, of the phone. 'Hello?'

'Yes, I am here. His name is Paul, why?'

'Well, Trish, he is the last person to see the girls and I need to talk to him.'

'Is he a suspect?'

'I don't know yet.' Mia hung up the phone and heard someone across the room shush everyone and ask for the T.V. to be turned up.

Breaking News!

What now?

A women has found dead at Hanging Rock, by people that were hiking the rock. They stood at the edge to have a look down at the gorgeous landscaping and rockery, only to see a woman's mangled body between tree's like someone threw her over.

'FUCK ME!' Mia whispered under her breath. Looking at the scene from the T.V., it looks like police had it covered. There was crime tape sealing of the tracks, media, and ambulance were all there. I can't investigate this right now; it may not be a link to the serial killer.

Mia rang Paul but there was no answer just a voicemail. 'Hi Paul, I am Mia Gauci, I am leading the case of the two missing girls Ava and Ivy. I would like to speak to you please, call me back ASAP. Thank you.'

Mia had an idea, dialling Jax's number she waited for him to answer. 'Hello,' answered Jax, sounding puffed out.

'Hello, Jax, it's Mia. Are you okay, have you been running?'

'No not running per say, but I did run out of the toilet to answer the phone.' They both laughed together.

'Hey, Jax what are you doing right now, do you have plans?'

'No, why?'

'I was thinking I would drive out to the last place the girls were and rang to see if you wanted to come along.'

'Yes, yes, of course. Okay, I am on my way.'

*　*　*

TOOTING THE HORN JAX came out, jumped in the car and they looked at each other again they felt some sort of connection, but said nothing.

'Okay, let's go,' Mia said finally.

It was a long drive and they played music, laughed together, and got to know each other.

'How long were you and Ava together, Jax?'

'Nine years. I fell in love with her the moment I saw her. We clicked straight up and that was it.'

'Just like we do,' said Mia. Oh my God! I can't believe that just came out of my mouth. Mia wanted the ground to swallow her up. Jax turned his head to look at her, and he started to look at her differently.

'Yes, Mia, just like we do.' They glanced at each other again. 'Well we are here, time flies when you are having fun. Jax, I am going to drive to the location of the party I know I can trust you with keeping all this to yourself, right?'

'Yes, of course.'

Pulling up at the end of the driveway, Mia turned to Jax, 'Okay, we need to follow where we think they went by car.' Mia did a U-turn to face the dirt road at the end of the driveway, 'Okay, let's drive slowly in case there are any roads we missed on the way in.'

They saw nothing for the first five minutes, then they noticed on the right the forest was more dense. They noticed a thinner track going into the forest, 'Should we go down there, Jax.'

'Yep let's go, but you might get scratches on your car.'

Off they go extremely slowly, crawling pace about 20 km. They were now deep in the forest, looking at each other.

'I have a bad feeling about this, Jax.'

'Yes, I am uneasy as well.' Driving another 5 minutes down the dirt track, Jax noticed a river flowing down the bottom of the mountain, as they were driving on the top of the mountain. Mia stopped the car and they got out to have a look. There was an eerie silence in the air, but the sounds of the forest animals and birds put them a little at ease.

'Jax, I wonder how people know this exists. This land, this river, anyone could be buried here. The wild pigs and foxes would eat the carcass of a human. I think I will send a search team up here; it is National park.' Getting back into the car they continued to drive.

'Where does this track lead, I wonder?' said Jax. Fifteen minutes more they drove and came to a fence and that was padlocked. A sign on the gate said, "private property KEEP OUT".

'Wow! You have got to be kidding me; someone owns property here.' Getting out of the car, they leant against the fence to see if they could see a house or sheds. Yes, they could see like a bunk house but it was so far in the distance they couldn't make out if anyone was there, or if it was occupied. 'Jax are you thinking what I am thinking?'

'That the girls could be in there?'

'Yes, they may be. Or it could just be someone's home.' Mia spontaneously yelled out, 'HELLO, IS ANYBODY THERE?'

'Are you mad, what if somebody is there we should not be here?'

'It just came out my mouth.' Silence was in the air. 'Jax I am going to get a smoke out of the car, do you want one?'

Jax's face was blank, 'Yes, I will.' Mia lit a smoke and gave one to Jax, who was still staring at her.

'What?'

'Would not have taken you for a smoker. I do not smoke all the time just now and then.'

'Me too,' said Jax.

'Well there you go. Jax, what are your thoughts on this place?'

'Well, it is ironically close to where they where last seen, this place is hidden from civilisation. Anything could go on here and no one would know about it. There is a feel in the air that just does not sit right with me anyway.'

'Yes, my thoughts exactly. Okay, let's start the drive back home.' Leaving the eerie forest behind, they played Jimmy Barnes music, sung and laughed some more. 'Jax what will you do if Ava is dead?'

'I don't know, I haven't thought of that yet. This is a situation I will have to take one day at a time. I know she is a strong woman, she is the strongest out of all her girlfriends.'

'Tomorrow I will start the search for the girls and document today privately.' They were close to home and the sun was going down. 'Are you hungry, Mia?'

'Yes, starving. Let's order takeaway and eat back at my house. What do you think?' Oh wow, this good-looking young man invites me to his house to eat, is it just that or is there something more this. We looked at each other with curious looks, what do I do?

'Yes, okay Jax. I will come over to eat, what do you want?'

'Pizza?'

'Yes, that is fine.' Mia and Jax were about thirty minutes away from home, they turned off the CD, put the radio on and the 8 pm news came on. The woman that was found off the highway, near Woodend, has been identified as Kim Brown, the other woman that has been found at Hanging Rock has been identified as Emma Miller.

'This is getting out of control, I have so much work going on all at one time. We must catch this bastard or bastards,' said Mia.

Jax piped up, 'The name Kim Brown sounds familiar to me, why do I know that name?'

'Hold on, Jax…'

'WOOOOH! FUCK! You drive like a mad woman.'

'I do when I need to go to the bottle shop,' she laughed. 'Do you want a drink Jax?'

'Yes, let get drinks.'

Mia walked out with a bottle of Vodka and Jax with Jack Daniel cans, smiling.

'Okay, we are set,' Mia said.

Arriving at Jax's home, the chilled night air was settling in. They put the heater straight on, and until the warmth of the canara heated the house, Jax lit the fire and the flames started to glow and give an ambient feel to the house.

'Make yourself comfortable, I will order the pizza.' Mia opened the vodka and poured lemon-lime bitters into it. In front of the canara, Jax had a Sherpa Prestige Rug. Mia sat on it, leaning her back against the couch, and placing the Vodka on the coffee table. Looking around the lounge room, Mia noticed pictures of Jax and Ava around the room in more happier times. Mia felt slightly uncomfortable and wondered if she should leave. Jax walked into the dim lit lounge room and stood there for a moment looking at the orange flame from the fire glowing across Mia's face.

Mia felt eyes on her, turned her head and looked at Jax willingly. 'Jax should I leave, is this right for me to be here?'

Jax said, 'I will be out in 10 minutes, pizza is ordered. Relax, if you do not feel comfortable, I will not hold you here.' Jax disappeared. Hmm, where did he go to? While Jax was not in the room, she took advantage of getting up and walking around the house. It was clean, neat, and in order. Ava has kept this house well. Walking out of the kitchen Mia could hear a radio playing from another room, following the music she came to a stop. It was coming from the bedroom ensuite. Shit, he is in the shower. Her heart was racing, she had a wonderful female partner at home waiting for her, but she was tempted to peek, and was curious to find out why her heart skips a beat when she was around Jax.

Should I peek? Creeping quietly and closely to the bathroom door, Mia poked her head in the crack of the door, she could not look away. Steam fogged up the bathroom, music was playing, and she watched Jax lather himself. Sudds were dripping down his muscular body, perfect buttocks, and solid six-pack. Mia felt wet. Why am I excited? I like women, why am I trying to convince myself? She was facing unanswered questions that she needed to think about. Mia's temperature skyrocketed, she felt hot so she had another swig of her drink.

In one moment, Mia screamed and fell through the bathroom door, Jax's dog that was outside came in the doggie door and frightened Mia. Feeling embarrassed she said, 'I am so sorry Jax, your dog scared me.'

Jax turned around in the shower and didn't say a word, just opened the door and held his hand out for Mia to grab. She grabbed his hand and got up of the floor, and he pulled her into the shower without words. He intensely started kissing her, fondling her breasts. Water was running over the both of them as Jax undressed her, running his hands over her body. She froze, as he looked at her deeply, caringly, arousing her soul just with his intense look. Fuck.

Mia could not hold back anymore, and she let herself be with Jax. He made mad, intense love to her in the shower. The shower turned off and Jax lead Mia with a blanket to the fireplace, still without words. He caressed her breasts, running his hands down her stomach towards her wet vagina, listening to her moaning, made Jax more excited. He kissed her passionately and made sweet love to Mia again.

'Wow! Jax, what just happened. No man has made me feel like this ever.' Jax smiled at her and said, 'You are an amazing, beautiful woman, Mia. I know you have a girlfriend, what you tell her, or do not tell her I will leave that to you.'

'I am starved, I have not heard the pizza man knock at the door, have you?'

'No, I am going to see if he left them outside, we did take a long time.' The laughed together. Opening the door, the pizzas were placed at the bottom of the door.

SURVIVAL

H UDDLED IN A CORNER, bleeding and scared, the girls heard a call out in the distance. Ivy tried to scream for help but no one heard her cries.

'Ava, someone is at the property calling out. It is the police looking for us. Why don't they come closer, is there only one or tow or more people are out there looking for us? Oh god where are we?'

The girls heard footsteps coming closer to the door of the trapped room they were in, squeezing each other tighter. The door flung open and before them were masked men, four of them.

'You, up now,' directed at Ivy.

Ivy started screaming and crying, 'No, please no. Don't hurt me.' The men heavily walked over and picked her up like a rag doll, still holding on to Ava's hand. They yanked them apart, while taking Ivy out of the room, Ivy screamed, 'I love you, Ava.'

Ivy could see they were underground somewhere, as they took her along cold, wet, darkened halls. Cobwebs everywhere hanging from the walls, down the hall were cell-like rooms. She saw dead girls, chained, rotted and left for dead. The last room she passed she saw Hannah, dead and hanging from the roof. Oh lord Jesus Christ, please let me survive this hell I have been placed into. Ivy recited all the prayers she could remember, in this time of panic. Lord I will go straight, if this is my punishment for not working a good, clean job. I will change, dear lord, please help me. No, this is not how it ends for me; I am not going out like this.

They stopped to open a door and placed Ivy on a table that was cold, hard metal, strapping her down at the ankles and wrists. Begging for her life, in a way Ivy knew it was the end, but she did not give up asking for them to release her. Ivy viewing the room, could see tools, tables with objects with blood all over them. The dimly lit room smelt of blood and death, Ivy also noticed camera's and computers, and saw a monitor with an internet live show ready to go live with a bidder's section. Shit, people are watching us getting raped, die and be decapitated, and paying money. Oh fuck! Sick fucks. Our lives are a gambling game to these sicko's, and they are dirty police officers too. I will never be able to tell Ava. My family will never know what happened to me. Oh Blade, I will never see your beautiful face again, we can never start the family we wanted so much.

Love you Mum and Dad, l love you too Blade.

'We are going live in five minutes,' one man said. "Put in your bid and tool of choice" came up on one of the computer screens. Oh god I see this shit in the movies, now I am at my death for real. This is the movie of my death.

Tears streamed down Ivy's face, there was nothing she could do, they had now gagged her.

The show went live, first bid was to see her raped.

Ripping off her pants, one man dropped his pants and forced himself into her. The ratings started going higher, and the higher they were getting the more excited he became and more rough it was for Ivy. Ivy was shaking her head which was all she could do and one man after another just continually raped her until they were all finished the ratings skyrocketed.

Someone else requested through the site that her nipples be bitten. They cut her top off and one man on each side of her started biting her nipples. Ivy's muffled screams were coming from behind her gag. Ivy was in extraordinary pain by now and wanted it to be over, but she knew this was going to be a long torture. Next they cut off her nipples and sliced cuts behind her ankles, so now she would not be able to walk even if there was a chance of escaping. Next her fingernails were ripped off one-byone. Her eyelids were cut off and during this Ivy had passed out. The pain was excruciating it was just too much for her to bear but she was still breathing and alive.

Then Ivy came to for a brief moment, saw a man standing close to her waist and felt a tool like a saw near her upper thigh and she knew her leg was about to come off. She looked into the man's eyes and in that moment she knew the eyes that she was looking into, they felt familiar the man looked at her and winked from behind his mask she knew she knew this man somehow. And then he started to saw her leg and she passed out again.

Blood poured out everywhere from Ivy's leg and her face where her eyelids were cut off, from her fingernails.

She was bleeding out from everywhere, within twenty minutes of them torturing Ivy, cutting off her leg, the men saw no movement and felt for a pulse. There was no pulse, Ivy had died.

The ratings from the live show with the highest they had ever been, and money was flowing into the sick game.

When they had finished with Ivy they moved the trolley down the hall, opened the door of the room that Ava was in and wheeled the trolley through the doorway. They pushed it into the room until it hit a wall and slam the door behind them.

* * *

AVA LOOK AT THE trolley and saw it was Ivy, decapitated and dead just blood just pouring out everywhere from her body. Ava leant against the wall and collapsed to the floor. In that moment she had never felt so alone, she had to come to grips with herself because if she didn't escape this would her fate, too. Ava cried a river, got it out of her system and then told herself that she needed to focus, looking around the room to find an escape hole.

There was no escape hole in this room, Ava hesitantly went over to the table Ivy was on, looking around and moving Ivy slightly to see if she could find any tools to use.

Under Ivy's head, to Ava's surprise, was a knife that had been used on Ivy. Ava could not believe her luck, now she had to plan on how she was going to use it. They are coming for me soon, I need to escape. I will stand behind the door and when it opens, I will stab someone in the neck, and hopefully that will occupy the man behind him. Then I will stab him too and run like hell down the halls to find an escape. Sure enough, she heard voices and footsteps, but not as many as last time. They probably thought because I was injured that I wouldn't put up a fight and the boss sent less men to come and get me.

Ava heard the men coming closer and closer to the door and she could hear that they were wrestling the door handle. Hiding behind the door with the knife up at head level, she was ready to make her move. The door came open and the men looked at the trolley that Ivy was on, one man said to the other, 'Where is the other bitch?'

As the first man proceeded to come through the door, Ava swung the knife and stabbed him through the neck sideways. Still having a good grip on the knife handle she pulled the knife out of his neck and he dropped to the ground bleeding out.

The man behind him yelled, 'What have you done you dumb bitch!' He started to kneel down to help his mate in need, but then realised Ava was approaching him and started to stand back up. Ava sliced his neck, this all happened in minutes, but to Ava it felt like hours. To her surprise there, was only two men. She ran through the door like mad. Running down halls which turned into tunnels, she knew she was underground and didn't know what direction the tunnels would take her in. All she could do was run for her life and hope for the best.

Injured and out of breath, not knowing where she was running to, Ava tried not to view the dead bodies lying around the halls and tunnels. She made a right turn through a tunnel that had water in the bottom of it, rats everywhere and the smell was the most awful smell she had ever smelt in her life.

She felt like vomiting but could not stop to do so. Ava had been running for around twenty minutes and she made another left into another tunnel, saw lights which looked natural so she ran towards it. Tt was a dead-end, looking up to the roof, where the light was coming from, there was a ladder. She climbed it as quick as she could in her condition and tried to force the opening open. It was like a hinged, heavy door she used all her power to lift it open. When she did and climbed through the opening, she noticed she was still in the forest. She ran like hell to a main road, tripping and falling along the way but not giving up.

Running for over an hour, Ava finally came to the highway and fell to the side of the road. Oncoming cars that had seen her drop had screeched their brakes to stop. Several cars pulled over and ran towards, her picked her up and put her in their car and took her to the Woodend hospital. Rushed into emergency, Ava was treated. At once the police were called to come down to the hospital to get a statement. By the time the police arrived at the hospital Ava was sedated and the police officers were asked to come back tomorrow.

The following day came the police offices went to the hospital to talk to Ava.

'Hello Ava, we know you have been through a rough ordeal, but we need to speak to you. Do you feel up to talking to us?'

'Yes, but not for long,' she replied. Ava was staring into space started saying 'they're dead, they are all dead.'

'Ava, who are all dead? Where abouts in the forest did you run out from, did you see anybody, did you see anybody that tortured you?'

'They wore masks, I could only see their eyes. One set of eyes looked familiar, I had no time to think of who they reminded me of. There were many men in masks. There are so many girls dead at the place I was captured. I am not talking one or two, I am talking a whole lot more when I escaped from the hole. I remember the track I took to get out, I can take you there when I have recovered.'

'Okay Ava, that is good. That will be enough for today, we will come back tomorrow and check on you. Is there anybody we can call for you? You may also hear from detectives that are on this case they will come by to ask you questions.'

Nodding her head, without notice, she fell asleep. The police officers did not get family contact numbers, because she fell asleep so quickly. They left, asking the nurse to inform the detectives to ask Ava to give them her family phone numbers.

Two days passed before detectives turned up at the hospital, which was a relief to Ava as she needed rest.

*   *   *

MIA WAS CALLED TO come into the office. Leaving Jax's house, they kissed and Jax said goodbye. Mia arriving at the office, and sat at her desk to open emails. One email said URGENT RESPONSE NEEDED.

Mia, go as soon as you get this email to the Woodend Hospital. A girl was found alive, she was kidnapped and assaulted. She may have the key to the killer/ killers behind the serial killer. Go and interview now.

Mia picked up her car keys from her desk and headed out of town towards Woodend. Two hours later she arrived, flashing her badge at the doctors, I need to speak with the survivor of the kidnapping.

'Right, come this way Ms Gauci.'

Walking down the halls, going into the intensive care unit. They bypassed several rooms and then arrived at one room at the end of the hall.

'The patient is in here, miss. Please do not take too long as she is still distressed.'

'Sure, I will not take too long.' Mia slid the curtain back and saw a girl lying on the bed staring out of the window.

'Hello, miss. My name is Mia Gauci, I am here to ask you a couple of questions I hope you do not mind?' Ava slowly turned her head toward the lady standing there, staring blankly at her face she saw that it was Mia standing at her bedside. Ava instantly felt comforted seeing a familiar face for the first time in a long time and started crying uncontrollably.

Mia's face went white as a ghost, she was expressionless, shocked it was Ava, Mia sat on the end of the bed and held Ava tightly as they cried together.

'Ava you are alive. I am so glad that you are alive and survived. Oh my God, what have they done to you girl?'

'They killed Ivy, Mia. There were more than ten dead girls where we were, Mia. I know these men are the killers, I just know it.'

'Okay, where were you held?'

'I do not know, but I can show you when I am better. I know how to get there.'

'Okay, I am just looking at your file that the doctors have made on your injuries. Fuck, Ava. So sorry you went through this. And I'm sorry about Ivy, we will get them now with your help.'

'Jax,' Ava said. 'Pardon?'

'Jax. I want to speak to Jax.'

Mia gulped and slightly flushed red, 'Sure I will call him and let him know you are here.'

'Blade, too,' Ava said. 'I need to see them both.'

Excuse me Ava I will make the calls for you; I will be just outside your room.

Jax heard his phone ringing and saw it was Mia. 'Hey Mia, you want some more of me huh?' There was silence on the other end. 'Hello? Mia?'

'Jax, I am at the Woodend Hospital.'

'What are you doing up there?' asked Jax.

'A girl had survived a kidnapping and was sent to the hospital, I am on the case since they think it may link to the serial killer.

Jax heard quick sharp breathing on the phone. 'Mia you are starting to worry me, what is up?'

'It's Ava, Jax. It'is Ava. She escaped her kidnappers; she wants to see you here with Blade. She is not in a good state, Jax.' Jax was now silent. 'Jax you there?'

'Yes, I am on my way. I will pick up Blade.'

'Okay, see you when you get here, I will stay with her until you arrive.' Jax hung up the phone and called Blade.

'Blade it's Jax. Can you come with me to see Ava she is alive at Woodend Hospital. Do you want me to pick you up?'

'No, I will meet you there I am not at home.'

Pulling up in the car park, Jax got out and as he closed the car door, he heard a voice say 'Hey, Jax. It was Blade.

'Hey Blade, she is alive. She's not good.'

'Bet you are happy to hear she's alive?'

'Yes of course.' They both walked fast into the Hospital, so fast it was like a slow jog.

'I am here to see Ava?' They all knew who Ava was and the nurse walked them to where she was. Knocking on the door, Ava, pulled back the curtain. Jax saw Mia sitting in the chair in the corner. He looked at her straight- faced then looked at Ava, stared into her eyes and he started to cry. They hugged like it was the first time they had met.

Mia had tears rolling down her cheeks watching the emotion of their reunion. Looking past Jax, Ava saw Blade.

'Come here sit on the bed. Blade I am sorry, to tell you this. Ivy is dead, Blade. What they did to her was awful, they tortured her so bad, that she bled out or died of shock, I don't know. But they threw her in the room I was in after they killed her, Blade. She had no eye lids, a leg was missing, she was torn below so I know they raped her.

I will always have that picture in my head of how she was tortured.' Blade sat motionless. 'Blade, are you okay?' As Ava tried to comfort him, she was looking into his eyes, at once she felt a cold chill, and recognised the eyes she saw under the mask. NO!

Starting to tremble and shake, the machines started buzzing and the nurses ran into the room.

'Okau everybody out please, she needs her rest. NOW.'

Ava grabbed hold of Mia's hand, suggesting she stay. The boys waited outside the room.

The nurses calmed Ava down, giving her water which settled her a bit. 'Mia, Blade, his eyes.'

'Ava what are you saying?'

'His eyes are familiar, he was where I was captured.'

'Ava you have been through a traumatic experience, you need rest.'

'No, no. Do not let him back in here.'

'Okay, do not get worked up, okay. Ava I am going to ask the Hospital to transfer you to Westland Hospital near home, are you okay with that?'

'Yes. Get me security outside my door.'

'Okay,' said Mia.

Mia walked over the guys, Jax was still stunned and upset for Ava, Blade had no emotion.

Mia thought to herself, how strong Ava's reaction was to Blade, and requesting security. Also noticing herself that Blade had no emotion, when he was just told his girlfriend was killed and cut into pieces.

'Blade, are you okay?' Mia asked.

'Yes, I am shocked I think. I have not known anyone to die before.' Not sure whether to believe him or not, she kept her mouth shut.

'Jaz can I have a minute to talk to you?' Mia and Jax stepped away. 'Jax do you think Blade's lack of emotion and the way Ava reacted to him was strange?'

'Yes, it is strange, if I found out that Ava was killed in that manner I would be a crying mess. Mia not to read anything into it, but I asked Blade if he wanted me to pick him up to come here and he said no, I am near the hospital I will meet you there.'

'What would he be doing up here, Jax, does he have family up here?'

'No, he does not.'

'Okay, he is a suspect. Jax regarding…'

'Stop, I know what you are going to say, what happens to us now Ava is alive?'

'Well, no I was going to say that I will not be telling April, my wife, and you do not need to tell Ava. I see the love she has for you, and I care for you, I want the best for both of you really. I'm happy, she is alive Jax. We will get these bastards, I promise you. What happened with us, stays with us, okay.'

'Yes, okay.'

'Okay I must go now and organise the ambulance to move Ava to Westland Hospital tomorrow and organise security for tonight. I will call you and catch up with you later, Jax.' Mia headed for her car and hit the highway.

Calling the office and asking to have undercover police tracking Blade's every move from tomorrow.

* * *

A NEW DAY BEGAN. Ava was moved to Westland Hospital; she was happy to be close to home. Ava had a view out of her window, the sun was shining, the birds were chirping, and she was happy to be alive. Ava self- reflecting on what she had just been through, the death of her best friend and the death of Ally, and the other girls killed at the dungeon of horrors. She was feeling better on this new day and she was hoping to be home by Friday. Ava figured two more days of rest and she would be good to go home.

Friday came and Jax came to the hospital to pick Ava up and take her home. It was at lunchtime they arrived home. Opening the front door, standing still in a moment glancing around the room, feeling relieved she was home.

Sitting on the couch, she turned the T.V. on, and saw her case was on the news of how she survived. She flicked through the channels but they were all the same. Ava started to hear a lot of noise at the front of the house, peeking out of the window there were media, cameras, and people everywhere setting up.

'Jax come here, get rid of the media on our front lawn.' Jax tried to go out the front but the media bombarded him with questions and didn't hear him yelling at them to leave. Jax just went back into the house.

'Jax why is there wine glasses near the fireplace?' Jax stood frozen and realised he forgot to clean up after Mia left, he wasn't expecting Ava to be alive let alone come home this week.

'I had a co-worker over, she was stressed out and asked if she could come over to talk as I was an outsider to her life. She wanted to vent babe.'

'Right!' She was suspicious as far as she knew this had not happened before, but the media occupied her in this moment. Jax flew to the bathroom and bedroom to make sure Mia didn't leave anything behind.

The following week came, and Mia rang Ava to see if she were up to going on that drive back to where she escaped.

'Yes, let's go.' Mia, Jax and Ava headed up the highway. At first it was silent but then the radio played good music to break the silence. Stopping at one of the servos for a quick bite for lunch and toilet stop, Ava came out of the toilets to find that Mia and Jax seemed to be talking and standing closer than they should have been. Disregarding the thought, they all jumped in the car and drove off.

Twenty minutes came and went, and Ava directed them to the dirt road to pull over. They all got out of the car, it seemed silent as there were no cars driving past. Mia lit a smoke, remembering the time her and Jax where here last.

As if he was on autopilot, Jax lit a smoke as well.

Ava, looked at him, 'Jax when did you start smoking?'

'Oh, um, I always have but not in front of you. Ava, I only have one every now and then.'

'Right. Follow me down this way, this is where I came out from. I do not know if you can drive there but I was running for nearly an hour I am sure.'

'Wow!'

Grabbing their water bottles, off they went, walking through the rough foliage of the forest, through trees around rocks, Mia out of nowhere bent over with her hand on her knees and vomited. They all stopped.

'Are you okay, Mia?'

'Yes, I haven't hiked in a while you know. I am a smoker is all. Not fit.' Coming to a fence line, Ava said, 'Here we are, there is a hinged door covered in grass and all the dead girls are down there and Ivy.' Tears streamed down her cheek as she relived her nightmare.

'Jax this is the place we came to the other week.'

'Yes, it is.'

'What? You both have been here?'

'Yes, Ava I asked Jax would come here with me, but we went to the driveway of the Commissioner's home where the party was and followed it out and we somehow ended up here, and we were screaming out hello is anybody there.'

'Jesus Christ Mia, that was you? I heard you. There is a lot of men working underground here, there's not many on top of the land. They stay mostly downstairs, underground killing the women, that's all I know.'

'Excellent job leading us here, we have the place, we have suspects now we need to contact the judge to get a warrant. We are thankful you are alive Ava. For you to get out of the place that you did required all your will power.'

'Let's get out of here,' Ava said, eager to leave.

Nearly at home after another long drive, Ava spoke and said, 'Mia when you go back there to arrest them I want to be there. I need closure and to see who killed all these innocent women.'

'I cannot take you, Ava. Police and S.W.A.T will be everywhere.'

'I don't care, I am coming.'

'Let me see what I can do.'

* * *

BLADE BEING TRACKED SHOWED up nothing, he was living a normal life, so they stopped tracking him. It took a week of planning and getting the warrant, Mia was heading the arrest, the entry on to the property, organising crews. Called a meeting and made sure all crews were aware of their positions. Mia excused herself for a moment. Five minutes later she came back into the room and said,

Right 7.00am we leave this office. Go home, get rest and get ready for a new day, we will get these bastards.'

Mia went home to rest, still not feeling well. She drank water and it seemed to help. She messaged Jax to be ready by 7.00am to meet at the station and to bring Ava. They were all anticipating the day ahead.

*   *   *

ALL CREWS MET AT the station, Jax and Ava turned up, in thick warm coats. It was a fresh, chilly morning. Mia strolled out of the station, saw Jax and Ava and started to walk over to them.

'Hi guys. We have everything ready to go and under control, we will end this serial killing today.' Jax asked Mia if he could go to the toilet before they left. ;Follow me, Jax.' They walked a little bit away from Ava, but she could hear them talking. She slowly walked closer without them knowing.

'Jax, I am pregnant.' Jax stood still in time. The world spun around him.

'What?'

'I am pregnant.'

'Oh, fucking Jesus, Mia. You're a lesbian and my girlfriend survived being kidnapped, how do we explain this? Oh hell what are you going to do, are you going to keep it?'

'Yes, I am going to come clean to April. If she leaves me, then she leaves me. After some time she may come to accept this child. I am keeping it, Jax. What you tell Ava is up to you.'

EXPECTING THE UNEXPECTED

'NO NEED TO TELL me anything, Jax. You thought I was dead, so you moved on so quickly. I thought I meant something to you, Jax.' Flushed and red faced, Mia said, 'Ava it wasn't like that.'

'Yes right. You both make me sick. Let's get on with the day, the quicker it ends for me the better.'

'FUCK! FUCK!' Jax was fuming as he was walking to the toilet. Walking back to the police cars, all were set to go.

Off they went out to the highway again, this time in the most awkward silence.

'Ava can we talk about this? PLEASE?'

'No, you can find somewhere else to sleep tonight, Mia and April will put you up,' said Ava, being sarcastic.

At that moment Mia thought of April and how she would take this news. April was the love of her life, have I just broken my life as I knew it?

'Okay guys. We need to focus on what we are about to do, can we leave this for later?'

'Yes much later, like never,' said Ava.

Arriving down the dirt road all crews stopped to gear up, in vests, guns, screens, tear gas, head protective gear and all the equipment they needed. Mia headed the team to the gates, one police officer cut off the padlock that was on the gate. The driveway was long so they slowly walked along the driveway, then Mia put her hand up to stop. They all stopped for a moment; Mia saw the door flip open in the distance, the escape door that Ava had cme out from. There were two men climbing out.

Staring at the men Jax said, 'What the fuck? Mia are you seeing what I am seeing?'

'No way it can't be. It just can't be.' In their sights were Blade and Tate coming out of the hole. Mia yelled out, 'Move now, go!'

All crews ran to position. Mia and Jax ran ahead to Blade and Tate. They saw them coming and started running, but the police that were behind the fence line got them and pinned them to the ground. They handcuffed them and made them lay there.

Both staring up at Jax, 'What the fuck guys, what is this?' They did not answer him.

The police, Mia and Jax went down the hole after Blade and Tate were put into the police car. Climbing down a ladder, it was dark when they reached the bottom. Putting on their torches they saw so many tunnels, worst of all was the smell.

Mia did vomit, and the others were dry reaching. It was the smell of many dead bodies. Walking fast through the tunnels, they came to the killing area and saw girls hanging from roofs, chained to loops in the walls, no beds, no toilets, death in every cage. It was a sight they would never forget.

ExpECTING THE UNExpECTEd

Police ran down and around all the tunnels and captured eight other men. Mia then came to the computer room and saw a website. She played it back and saw it was live murder T.V.. She vomited again.

Sick bastards. The whole place was a crime scene now. Coming out of the hole with relief looking at all the arrested, Mia saw that five of the men where police officers. She couldn't believe her eyes, scanning them one by one. The Commissioner was included, he was the ringleader. Looking at the last man, she thought, Oh no! Rise you're in this too? Why? People trust the police we do this job to look after people, not harm them. Oh god why?

Heading back to Melbourne and leaving the forensics at the scene. They were all locked up. Media was frenzied at police station.

What a day. Jax hired a motel. Mia went home to confront April about having a fling with a man and falling pregnant. Stunned and speechless, April chose to be alone for a few hours to process the information.

The next morning, Jax left the motel and went home to talk to Ava, there must be a way for her to forgive me. Knocking at the door there was no answer. He used his key to get in.

'Ava, it's me, Jax. We need to talk.' No sound. She must be sleeping. Jax walked into the bedroom. No Ava, where is she? Going through the whole house – no, nothing. I will check to see if her car is here. He went out to the garage.

'NO, NO, NO, NO, BABE!' Jax ran over to Ava's body hanging by a rope from the garage roof, trying to hold her legs up. He tried to ring Mia at the same time.

'Mia get over here NOW! Ava has hung herself.'

Mia was there in a heartbeat. They got her down and laid her on the ground. Both cried in each other's arms. Mia called back up to get to the house. 'This is not how it's supposed to end, Mia. She survived so much to be alive, why this? Did we do this to her?'

'No, Jax. You can't think like that. How does it end, Jax?'

Jax felt this question was personal, 'What do you mean? Did you talk to April?'

'Yes, Jax she left me.'

'I am sorry, Mia.'

'It is what it is, Jax.'

*   *   *

A WEEK LATER IT was Ava's funeral. Jax said his apologies and goodbyes.

All the men involved with the killings of young adult industry workers were sentenced to death for the worst serial killing spree in history.

They claimed they were nothing but sluts and had no use in this world. There was a major Police investigation on the corrupt police officers.

Jax turned up at Mia's home knocked on the door. It surprised Mia. 'Let's start a new chapter, Mia and a new life. What do you say?'

'I thought you would never ask.'